SAWYER

GUARDIAN GROUP SECURITY TEAM BOOK 4

BREE LIVINGSTON

Sawyer: Guardian Group Security Team Book 4

Copyright © 2023 by **Bree Livingston**

Edited by Kristina Teele

Cover design by Book Covers for $30

http://www.facebook.com/stunningcovers

All rights reserved. No part of this publication may be reproduced, distributed or transmitted in any form or by any means, without prior written permission.

Bree Livingston

https://www.breelivingston.com

Publisher's Note: This is a work of fiction. Names, characters, places, and incidents are a product of the author's imagination. Locales and public names are sometimes used for atmospheric purposes. Any resemblance to actual people, living or dead, or to businesses, companies, events, institutions, or locales is completely coincidental.

Sawyer: Guardian Group Security Team Book 4 / Bree Livingston. -- 1st ed.

ISBN: 9798866169146

"A hero is someone who has given his or her life to something bigger than oneself." -- Joseph Campbell

1

Meesha Kingston wrinkled her nose as she pulled a glittering lime green cocktail dress off the clothing shelf in a small boutique in Greenville, North Carolina. "Meh." It was pretty and eye-catching, but it'd make her look like a tall Sour Patch Kids.

Her sister, Kayleigh, looked up, shook her head, and did the same nose wrinkle. "Oh, no. Not your color."

With nearly a year to find the perfect dress for her high school reunion, she'd been unhurried, but faster than she expected, her time had run out. Now she was in a frantic, last-minute rush because she had a flight to Miami to catch in less than twenty-four hours. Since there'd been no luck in Myrtle Beach, South Carolina, she'd driven the little over three hours to Greenville, North Carolina, hoping her sister, Kayleigh, could help.

Pulling another dress from the rack, Meesha grumbled under her breath and put it back. This dress needed to be perfect, especially since her high school rival, Anna Mears, would also be on the reunion Caribbean cruise. Much like high school, they'd butted heads at least once during each planning committee video call.

Not only did she gush about her perfect life as a fashion designer in New York, but five months ago, she'd met the love of her life because, of course, she had. It was one more thing Meesha didn't have, and she'd snapped, claiming she'd met a nice guy too. It wasn't love at first sight, but she had high hopes.

With each call, she'd refused to put the shovel down. There was no harm until two weeks ago, when Anna said she was sure her boyfriend would propose by the end of the cruise. Without so much as a blink, Meesha had opened her big mouth, and said her boyfriend would come with her too. It was too soon for a proposal, but he couldn't go nearly two weeks without seeing her.

The call had ended, and the hole she'd dug was so deep there was no getting out of it. No way was she admitting she'd lied the whole time. She'd been vague about his looks, so at least in that regard, she'd been smart. She'd immediately logged into her Mr. Matchmaker account and put out a call for a fake boyfriend. Single was the only requirement, and they'd get an all-expense paid trip to the Caribbean.

The next couple of weeks, she met guy after guy, finally settling on Glen Hughman. He'd won mostly because he was available, and she was so unattracted to him there was no chance for anything more. She'd also failed to mention her elaborate lie to her sister, and she was keeping it that way. Knowing her sister and her curiosity—and the fact that she worked at Guardian Group, a private security firm based out of North Carolina—Meesha was also smart enough to have Glen book his trip separate from hers.

"Oh, I like this purple." Kayleigh lifted the dress so Meesha could see it.

She eyed it for a moment, eventually shaking her head. "No, too dark."

Kayleigh sighed. "What's really going on? I get wanting a nice dress, but this feels like it's something deeper."

"I..." What did she say? That she didn't want to feel like a loser? It'd been ten years, and her teaching position in Paris was old news after her ex-boyfriend, Noel Petit, had ripped it from her. At twenty-seven, what exactly did she have to show for herself since she graduated? A big, fat goose egg. "I just…I don't want to be a loser Kayleigh."

Kayleigh walked around the rack and faced her. "Meesha, you're not a loser. You're a fantastic teacher. The kids in Myrtle Beach love you. I know because I see all the little things they bring you, telling you they love you. You taught in France at a prestigious school, and it wasn't your fault you had to quit."

She gave a small shrug. "I know. Anna just gets to me. I've always come in second, and just once I'd like to be first." She turned her attention to the rack and gasped. "Look at this one." She pulled out a dusty blue sleeveless dress with a V-neck and flowing skirt and held it against her. "Oh, I like this one, and it hits just above my knees." At five-eleven, it was hard to find dresses that hit just right.

"Oh, my gosh, I love it too." Her sister gushed.

"Okay, this gives me five dresses to try on. One of them must be it." She walked with Kayleigh to the dressing room she'd used to hang her other four picks while she looked for the fifth, and slipped inside.

The first dress wasn't all the way on before she took it off. "Nope. It's pretty, but it's not pretty on me. Rose is not my color."

"Aw, I liked that one."

"Well, it didn't like me at all." A montage of trying on dresses played in her head, and she grimaced.

Instead of leaving the dusty blue until last, she grabbed it and slipped it over her head, grinning as the soft fabric fell into place. She pulled the door open and stepped out. "I love it."

Kayleigh had taken a seat a few feet away, and her mouth dropped open as she pushed out of the chair. "Oh, my goodness." She closed the distance, fluffing one of the flowy panels on the skirt. "The wide cinch at the waist accentuates your figure so well. If I didn't know any better, I'd say it was made specifically for you."

Meesha twirled, the skirt flaring out. "I feel pretty and confident in it. And it's super comfortable." She turned one way and then the other, placing her hand on her stomach. It was the prettiest dress she'd ever tried on. Her ocean blue eyes seemed to pop, and it even worked with her dark brown hair. "It's perfect, and I already have some sandals that will go with it." She exhaled in relief. That saved some time too, now that she wouldn't be shopping for shoes. "This gives me enough time to get home and finish packing."

"Okay, well, Tru and I are paying for it. So—"

"What? No, I can pay for it," she scoffed. "I mean… I appreciate it, but you guys don't have to do that."

Oh, how she wanted a relationship like her big sister. Tru was a wonderful man, and their entire family loved him. The affection he poured on Kayleigh was enviable. They hadn't met under the greatest circumstances, but no one could deny that they loved each other.

If only Meesha could find a guy like him. Sweet, kind, protective, and loving. She wanted to look a man in the eyes, say those vows of loyalty and long-lasting, long-suffering love. The kind that held a person up when they were weak and cheered a person on as they ran the race. Relationships weren't easy, but with the right guy next to her, they could weather storms and build a future together.

At least, that's what she hoped she'd have one day. Although, her last relationship had left her seriously gun-shy. He'd seemed so great at the beginning. Eight months later, it'd ended with her life turned upside down and so unsure of herself that she hadn't even attempted to date. And that was exactly why she'd picked Glen. Zero chance of a romantic connection.

A smile lifted her sister's lips. "We're not taking no for an answer."

Meesha groaned. "I feel bad when you guys pay for things."

Her sister shrugged. "We know things are tight with you working for such a small salary. It's the first time you're going somewhere that we won't be right there, and we just want you to have a good time with a little extra spending money during port stops."

She hugged Kayleigh. "Thank you."

When she'd returned from France, Guardian Group suggested protection, but she'd declined. There didn't seem to be a need when Noel was on a travel ban. Another kind offer from Ryder Whitaker's wife, Kennedy. Learning she'd survived similar situations made it infinitely easier for Meesha to talk to her, too.

Five months later, she was confident enough to move out of Kayleigh's place to Myrtle Beach, a town that was a hop and a skip away. It gave her just enough space to feel like she was on her own without being so far away in case anything happened.

Kayleigh held her out by her arms, smiling ear to ear. "I'm so proud of you. You are so strong and beautiful, and one day, you're going to meet the guy of your dreams. Until then, no one is rushing you either. Okay?"

Smiling, Meesha nodded. "I know, and thank you." She slipped inside the dressing room and quickly took the dress off and handed it to Kayleigh as she used the door to cover herself. "I'll be right out."

"Okay, see you up front."

After dressing, she met Kayleigh at the store's entrance, and together they walked to the car. They'd agreed that if they found the dress quick enough, they'd have a super-fast late lunch before she headed back to Myrtle Beach.

As Meesha got in the car, her phone rang. Thinking it was Glen, she answered without checking the caller ID. "Hey Glen, what's up?"

"Mon amour, my Meesha."

My love? My Meesha? Noel? Her stomach twisted. She'd changed her provider, her number, and used a VPN. How had he found her?

Meeting Noel Petit had wrecked her life. They'd met at the Louvre during a school event, and he'd been so wonderful and charming at first. Eight months later, when she broke it off, he began stalking her. In the end, she'd made the tough decision to give up her position to get as far away from him as possible.

Meesha scrambled out of the car, spinning in place, scanning the area for him. "Noel, why are you calling me? We've been over for a year now."

"I wish I had the time to tell you, but since your sister seems to be alarmed, we'll have to talk another time. Perhaps you can wear that blue dress."

The line went dead as Kayleigh's head popped up over the hood of the car. "Was that Noel?"

Nodding, Meesha slowly met her sister's gaze. "He knew you were in the car with me, and that my dress is blue."

Kayleigh's eyes widened and her mouth dropped open. "He's here?"

"I...I don't think so. He was on a travel ban to the states."

Her sister mulled the information for a moment. "Let's go to Guardian Group and speak to Ryder and Mia. If Noel is here, they'll find him."

Meesha's heart sank. If they couldn't find Noel, they'd pressure her to cancel her trip. After spending so much time and money on it, it made her want to cry. Kayleigh just wanted her safe, and while she understood that, giving Noel one more thing made Meesha sick. He'd taken her job, forced her to move back to the states. If he took this, she wasn't sure she'd recover.

A fire of determination lit in her belly. No, he wasn't going to rip this trip from her. She wasn't going to let him. Whether Ryder and Mia found him or not, she was still going on her cruise. It was a risk she was willing to take.

2

Sawyer James knocked on Noah Wolf's slightly ajar door and paused, waiting for his boss's permission to enter. Working at Guardian Group Security Firm over the past year had given him a sense of purpose, something a twenty-nine-year-old needed when he was desperately trying to atone for murder. Well, that was his opinion and he'd yet to find anyone to convince him otherwise.

Years ago, the group was formed by Pamela Williams when she lost her husband in a drive by shooting. After his death, she found out he'd left her a sizeable fortune. To keep his memory alive, she started it with the goal of helping people who had nowhere else to turn, regardless of their wealth. When she found love again, she handed the reins to Noah, who had been running the group ever since.

"Come on in," Noah called.

Sawyer pushed the door open a little wider, confronted with walls filled with photographs that spoke more than a thousand words of love, devotion, and happiness. He shoved the longing aside and reluctantly retreated to the reality of his situation. At least he'd earned enough of his teammates' trust that they allowed him to help them with their kids when they needed an extra pair of hands.

Finding Tru sitting to the left of Noah was a bit of a surprise. Usually when he was given assignments, it was a one-on-one meeting with Noah, and maybe Ryder or Mia so they could fill in the finer details if needed. If it were a full-team response, they'd meet in the conference room.

"Uh, hey, Noah. Hey, Tru." He stepped closer to Tru and shook his hand. "Good to see you. Did you and Kayleigh enjoy Okinawa?" The Truman Dynamic duo were Guardian Group's secret weapon. It was easy for them to go in looking like an ordinary couple and bring back intel that aided in missions.

Tru grinned. "We did and got a little information along the way."

Sawyer wouldn't ask any more questions. Sometimes they were working on cases that were need-to-know and it wasn't his business. "Well good. Tell Kayleigh those chocolate chip cookies of hers didn't last a day." She sure could bake, and he never turned down homemade goodies.

"You can tell her yourself. She should be here shortly." The tone seemed to imply that a situation was brewing.

Sawyer looked from him to Noah. "Everything okay?"

"Tru's taking lead on this," Noah said, pushing out of the chair. "I'm going to get the conference room set up and then check on Ryder and Mia."

"Thanks Noah," Tru said.

With a two-finger salute, their boss left his office.

Sitting back, Tru stretched his legs out and crossed them at his ankles. "Kayleigh's baby sister, Meesha, may need some help. She was teaching in France roughly three years ago. While there, she met this guy named Noel Petit, and dated him for roughly sixteen months. From what I understand, he was a bit of a mooch, living off his dad's money, and enjoying the perk of being a politician's kid. When she broke it off, he began stalking her and eventually got arrested trying to break into her apartment. She got an order of protection and no-contact, and he was put on a travel ban."

Sister-in-law. Teacher. France. Abusive ex-boyfriend. "All right."

"Kayleigh texted me about twenty minutes ago

telling me he'd called Meesha. During that call he told Meesha he knew my wife was sitting in the car with her, and the color of the dress they'd just purchased. Of course, that spooked both of them."

"Was he there?" asked Sawyer.

Shaking his head, Tru said, "They did a quick glance around and didn't see him, but Kayleigh knows better than to go after a suspect without backup. She immediately called me, I called Ryder and Mia, and Kayleigh and Meesha headed this way."

Sawyer's eyebrows knitted together. "Think maybe he was using the cameras at the shopping center." No doubt the place had them. With the current state of the world, it wasn't a logical leap.

"I don't know. Maybe. I've only heard bits and pieces about the situation from Kayleigh. Meesha was stingy with information when she got back to the states. I'm pretty sure she's not told us everything. She did get counseling from Kennedy, but of course, she can't share their conversations."

Kennedy was a sweet natured woman who ran Pets for Vets, a charity that matched veterans with emotional support animals. She'd offered Sawyer counseling too, but he didn't need it. He knew what he'd done, and no amount of talking about it would change it. Ryder sang her praises, describing how hard she'd fought for him. Sawyer still declined. The situations weren't the same.

Exhaling, Tru straightened. "The only thing I know about Noel is that his dad is some high-up in the French government."

Why did that not surprise him? "Do you think he'd pull strings to get Noel off the travel ban?"

Tru shrugged. "Maybe, I don't know." He paused. "We've now arrived at the tricky part."

"What's that?"

"Meesha leaves on a ten-day cruise tomorrow for her ten-year high school reunion. Again, I've gotten bits and pieces from my wife, but according to her, Meesha was on the planning committee, and it was a serious headache dealing with one of the other organizers. I'll bet a year's pay, she'll fight tooth and nail to go on that trip."

Rubbing his knuckles along his jaw, Sawyer whistled. "Well, I can definitely see that being a point of contention."

"A big one. I foresee a knock-down, drag out between Kayleigh and Meesha. Kayleigh isn't going to want her to go, and Meesha…" Tru chuckled. "Let's say she's got a level of determination that is nearly unmatched. That's as diplomatic as I can make it. I love her though. She's incredibly kind-hearted and sweet.

You ever need someone to fight for you, you call her. That's why her students and their parents love her."

Laughing, Sawyer grinned. "Has she met Britney Wells?"

That woman was a force of nature, for sure. When he'd met her, he'd known why Hendrix fell in love with her. They were a team and fought for each other. If Sawyer was looking, which he wasn't, he'd be looking for those character traits. Feminine, graceful, and full of fire.

While he loved Kayleigh like a sister, she was more subdued. Not in a bad way, but Tru and Kayleigh both came from loving, supportive families. Love came easy to them, and that was an unfamiliar world for Sawyer. Not that Tru and Kayleigh had an easy start, far from it, but they'd worked through it and made a life together.

Tru laughed, shaking his head. "Not yet, but I have a feeling they'd be good friends." He crossed his arms over his chest as the laughter died. "We're going to try to get Meesha to cancel her cruise. We don't know where this guy is, how long he's been following her, or what his plans might be. If he can get her number, there's a good chance he can get other information, like a ten-day cruise."

"I'm going to take a leap here and assume you want me to take the assignment?"

Nodding, Tru said, "Yeah, I'd like you to."

"Helps that I'm the only one available too." Sawyer laughed. It was a joke coated with regret. If only he could go back.

Tru grinned. "Even if you weren't, I'd still ask you because I trust you. I know you'll keep her safe."

That was high praise coming from a guy like Tru, especially since he knew a little of Sawyer's past.

"So, will you take her case?" asked Tru.

Nodding, Sawyer shook his hand. "Yes, sir, I sure will. You have my promise that I'll keep her safe too."

In Guardian Group, a promise wasn't thrown out like parade candy. A promise wasn't broken unless there was no other choice, and even then, it'd take more than a bullet or broken limbs. That was one of many things on a long list of reasons he loved his job.

Tru's phone rang, and he answered it. "Hey, sweetheart… Okay, we'll be in the conference room when you get here." He ended the call. "They've got about another ten minutes before they arrive, and by the sound of it, Kayleigh's been in a battle the entire drive here."

They stood and walked to the conference room. Noah was in his usual seat at the head of the table with a folder laid out in front of him so he could take notes with Mia and Ryder sitting across from each other, flanking him.

Mia looked up as Tru took a seat next to Ryder. "We can't find him," she said. "Granted we haven't been working on it long, but just a quick google brings nothing up. No social media, no pictures from events or functions. The last photo I found was dated a little over a year ago."

Ryder huffed. "I put a call into a friend there, and the records are sealed. Before I break into them, I'll reach out and request the information just in case we need to play nice."

Sawyer looked at Tru. "The records are sealed?"

"Yeah," Ryder said. "I found it odd too."

Mia nodded. "His dad isn't just in the French government either. He's a major player with power and influence. He's well liked, has extensive connections in various industries, and deep enough pockets to move mountains whether it's legal or not. His bank account makes Noah look like a pauper."

Noah looked at Mia, a shocked expression on his face. "Really?"

Sawyer's eyebrows hit his hairline. He whistled. That was a lot of money then because Noah was a billionaire. His family owned a computer parts distribution company, and they were all well-to-do. Good, salt-of-the earth people though. By the way the man acted, no one would ever guess it.

Tru grunted. "Are we assuming he's the one who had the records sealed?"

Mia nodded. "Yeah, possibly, but the little I've gathered, Noel and his father don't get along very well. The mother dotes on him though, so it could be her or she could have influenced dad to do it."

A ding went off and Ryder looked at his laptop screen. "Well, first search finished. He's not in any of the hospitals or psychiatric facilities there in France. I'll go ahead and expand the search."

Raised voices filtered from the hallway, and a moment later, Kayleigh burst into the room, instantly looking in Tru's direction. "She's actually fighting me on this."

With her hands on her hips, Meesha faced off with Kayleigh, putting her back to Sawyer. "There's nothing to talk about. I'm going."

Sawyer angled his chair away, so he didn't stare at how well Meesha filled out her jeans because, boy, did she.

"Meesha, he called you. He knew I was in the car with you and the color of your dress. This is madness."

Tru tipped his head in their direction. It was guy-speak for *let me break that up and introduce you*.

When Tru reached Kayleigh, he wrapped his arms around her, and kissed the top of her head. "Time out."

He motioned to Sawyer. "Meesha, I'd like to introduce you to Sawyer James. Sawyer, this is my little sister, Meesha." It wasn't lost on him that in-law was missing.

Meesha turned and Sawyer's breath caught as their eyes met with a shockwave nearly rocking him back on his feet. A vision played in his mind of diving into those two pools of ocean blue and forgetting his troubles. Her height was a positive physical trait too. He was six-two and she had to be at least five-ten and perfect for kissing. Her dark hair fell in waves well past her shoulders, and as shiny as it was, he was sure it'd feel like satin if he ran his fingers through it.

Without a doubt, she was the most beautiful woman he'd ever seen... and his friend's little sister which meant he needed to stop gawking because she was completely off-limits. He stuck his hand out. "Hi, it's nice to meet you."

Her luscious pink lips lifted into a smile, she slipped her hand in his, and he was certain the whole room heard the pop. He jerked his hand back as an electrical current raced up his arm, down into his gut, and spread through his body like wildfire. "Sorry, I tend to shuffle my feet too much." It was the lamest of lame excuses, but it was all his brain could muster. He'd met plenty of attractive women before, and that was a first.

She giggled, tucking a piece of hair behind her ear. "That's okay. It's nice to meet you too." Her gaze dipped to the floor, and she caught her bottom lip in her teeth. "Do you always go barefoot?"

"Anytime I can. Can't stand shoes."

"When I was teaching in Paris, I had a little girl in my class. She despised shoes. I talked the parents into using it as a way to get her to focus on her work. I've never seen a child work so fast in my life." She laughed and this one was even better than the giggle.

Sawyer shrugged. "If it works. Guess I should have had you as a teacher. Maybe I'd have graduated with better than a C."

"Grades aren't everything," she said as she stuck her hands in her back jeans pockets and rocked on her feet. "They're not the only measure of a man."

Have mercy. "Aw, well, I'd fail that one for sure."

Her gaze roamed his face, and her eyes found his once again, narrowing a fraction. His mouth went dry, and the air was thick between them. It felt like she was digging through the baked-on dust covering his soul. Finally, she tilted her head, saying, "No, that is absolutely not true."

Catching his gaze, she held it until his pulse rocketed. If he had a collar on, he'd be tugging on it. "No. No, I don't think so," she said.

What shocked him more than the statement was the tiny sprig of fragile hope. In the back of his mind, he could hear the voices of the people who'd rallied a defense for him. His head was telling him to shut those shouts out while his heart tried to smother the logic.

Noah cleared his voice, breaking the little bubble he'd found himself in. While he was flirting with Meesha, Tru and Kayleigh had taken their seats and they'd witnessed the whole thing along with everyone else at the table. He wasn't interested in romance. He knew his fate in the world so what was the point in torturing himself. He knew it, the people at the table knew it, and they'd just witnessed his downfall. He was almost positive he'd never be able to look a single one in the eyes again.

Throwing his thumb over his shoulder, he nodded toward the group gathered. "Seems their ready to talk and see what options there are at the end."

Another soft giggle with the hint of a blush covered her cheeks. "Okay."

He stuck his hands in his pockets as he followed Meesha to the table. On his way, he glanced up just long enough to verify his theory. Yeah, based on the goofy grins, he was never going to live this down.

It'd been years since he'd flirted like that with a woman. One second he was saying hello, and the next, all he could see was her. If he hadn't already told—no promised—Tru he'd take the assignment, he'd be tucking tail and running.

She sandwiched herself between Tru and Kayleigh. "Hey guys," Meesha said.

Ryder smiled and Mia waved.

"Hey Meesha," Noah said. "I know it's a pain but start from the beginning. Don't leave anything out, even the small details. You'd be surprised how much it helps."

Nodding, she caught her lip. "Okay." She cut her eyes to Sawyer and quickly looked away but not before he caught a blanket of pink covering her cheeks. Talk about an interesting reaction.

No way. None of those sorts of thoughts needed to be floating in his head either. Tru and Kayleigh trusted him to protect her and that was it. He wasn't going to do anything to break that trust either, including making googily eyes at their sister.

Besides, she'd be a client if she accepted their help. Sure, the other guys had fallen in love with clients, and Hendrix had even married Noah's sister. No matter what Hendrix said, though, their situations weren't the same. He'd been a hurt, neglected kid lashing out, while Sawyer was an adult.

Despite his thoughts, he could see a threaded needle making the initial stitch and the fabric marker laying down the guide that would end with his heart permanently sewn to hers. He could *no* and *nope* all he wanted, but something had happened.

Shaking his head, he forcibly pushed the image away. He'd keep his promise to Tru and keep her safe, and that was all he was going to do.

3

Sandwiched between Kayleigh and Tru, Meesha stole another glance at Sawyer James. Holy smokes he was hot. She didn't believe in love at first sight, but she had to admit she was drawn to him. She'd been so angry when she walked into the conference room, she hadn't even noticed him at first. In her mind, it was an arrestable offence for failing to immediately acknowledge such a fine specimen of a man.

When she'd turned around, she'd nearly swallowed her tongue. His gorgeous crystal sea-green eyes met hers, and she was positive he'd walked down from Mt. Olympus. With thick, shaggy blonde hair that curled around his ears, it was all she could do to resist the temptation to run her fingers through it. An urge she was still finding difficult to ignore. Typically, the scruffy, five o'clock shadow wasn't her thing, but he wore it so well, she didn't mind at all.

His t-shirt and jeans seemed to match his casual, laid-back demeanor. That poor shirt was stretched as far as the fabric would go, and he filled out a pair of jeans better than any man she'd ever seen. Tall, well-built with arms like cannons, they left no room for doubt that when he held a woman, she knew it.

Wrapping the entire package together like a bow, a lady-killer smile on his oh-so-kissable lips made her knees go weak. If Guardian Group sold posters, she'd be stopping at the gift shop on her way out.

Kayleigh bumped her arm. "Noah's talking to you."

Meesha jumped and her cheeks heated. "Oh, sorry." That electric handshake with Sawyer had left her brain fried. She could still feel zings racing up her arm. His excuse of static electricity wasn't exactly what she would have called solid either. His red cheeks had tattled on him.

"It's okay." Noah said. "I know it's a pain but start from the beginning. Try to give us as many details as possible. The more Ryder and Mia have, the better."

She nodded and launched into the tale. "We met at the Louvre. They were having a fundraising event and all the teachers at my school were invited. He seemed like a normal guy, attractive and charming." She smiled as she recalled the night. "It was like something out of a movie. We hit it off immediately. He invited me to take a walk when the event ended. We strolled around Paris until our feet hurt and then we stopped at a little outdoor café. We talked all night. It was like I'd known him forever. The sun was coming up when he walked me home. That was it; I was smitten."

It'd been the best night. After everything she'd been through, she still looked back on that night with fondness. Casting her gaze to her lap, she sighed. "Over the next six or so months, we spent every free moment together, and then he invited me to meet his parents. Although, I found it odd because when he talked about them, I got the impression they didn't get along at all. I didn't know at the time his family was wealthy or that his father was in government."

"Did his father like you?" asked Noah.

"Oh, yes, especially when he found out where I worked. Creepily so. You'd thought I'd walked on the moon or something. They praised Noel for finding such a lovely woman." She held up her hands. "Their words not mine."

Lowering her gaze to her lap, she replayed the memories. "That's when things began going downhill, at least in retrospect. That next week, he called me every day, flowers were showing up at the school and my apartment. I finally had to tell him to stop, or I could lose my job."

While she paused for Noah to catch up with his note taking, she flicked her gaze in Sawyer's direction. It was supposed to be a quick look, but those pools of crystal green were trained on her. Not in a lecherous way. It felt more like he was giving her his undivided attention, as if he were taking mental notes. Slowly his lips quirked in a smile and flames raced up her neck to her ears. She jerked her attention back to Noah and the second he stopped writing, she continued.

"Almost every weekend we went to a cultural event or a party. When I wasn't available, Noel would get so upset. I brushed it off because the longer I spent time around Noel and his parents, it was obvious that he'd been subjected to some sort of abuse. Maybe not physically, but definitely emotionally and mentally."

She leaned forward with her arms on the table. "I will say, it seemed like the longer I dated Noel, the better his parents treated him. It was harder and harder to be around them too, but as weird as it was, Noel was happy. He seemed to soak up the affection, and I didn't want to take that away from him."

Sawyer chuckled. "That's different." What a voice. It was a lullaby for her ears, deep, warm, and soothing like a heated blanket. He could read the phonebook, and he'd have her undivided attention. His laugh was great too. Their gazes locked, and once again, she was taken aback at the sorrow in them.

They'd been openly flirting, and she'd said there were more ways to measure a man. His eyes had clouded over, and he'd said he'd fail. If Tru called Sawyer a friend, there was no way he'd fail. It made her wonder what could have possibly happened to make him feel that way. All she felt was a sweet spirit and a kind soul.

"You have no idea. It was so strange. I couldn't understand it," Meesha said.

Tilting his head, Sawyer asked, "When did things start going downhill?"

"The longer we dated, the more obsessive he became. I felt like I was tied to him constantly. If I wanted to meet friends for dinner, he'd complain. He wanted to know who I called, when I called them. It was like he wanted to itemize my day. It was so overwhelming."

Kayleigh covered Meesha's hand with hers and squeezed it before pulling it back. She appreciated the sweet show of comfort and support.

"One evening, when I was leaving school, a friend and fellow teacher stopped me. When I first arrived in Paris, she was the first person to welcome me. We were good friends. She needed to talk, and we went to dinner. I thought we would be talking about her, but then she started asking questions. By the end of dinner, I realized that I'd been isolated from my friends, I'd stopped calling my family, and doing anything that I might want to do. It woke me up."

Noah scribbled a few more notes down. "That's when you broke up with him?"

"Yeah, we had a huge fight. He was furious, accusing me of cheating on him, lying to him. I was exhausted. I couldn't live like that anymore. He began stalking and harassing me after that. It didn't matter what I did, he wouldn't leave me alone."

Noah scribbled a few lines of notes and lifted his head. "What made you return to the states?"

"He followed me home one day, begging to talk to me. When I wouldn't let him in the apartment, he started breaking the door down."

He'd done more than break down her door, but no one knew about that part. She'd left out the part where he'd hurt her. They also didn't know that she'd stayed in France long enough to recover from it before telling them she'd put in her notice.

"My neighbor saw what was happening and called the police. After that, I knew I couldn't stay. Even with the order of protection and no-contact, Noel wouldn't stop. Once the travel ban was ordered, I knew the only way to really get away from him was moving back."

Tru leaned back in his chair, angling it towards her. "Do you think he could be here?"

She shrugged. "I think he just wants to scare me. If he was here, he wouldn't have hidden himself. He would have made sure I knew he was around. A faceless call isn't his style."

Kayleigh turned to her. "I think you're underestimating him."

"His dad is heavily connected to many in the French government. What are the chances he found a way to help Noel out of the country?" asked Tru.

Meesha took a deep breath. "Honestly, I doubt it. When Noel and I went to events or parties, especially with those involving the elite circles, his dad introduced Noel with a few nice words. His parents would introduce me, and they'd practically fawn over me. More than once, it felt like Noel was jealous. I'd tell him no. They were just happy he'd found someone who cared about him, and they were being supportive."

"Did you really believe that?" asked Sawyer.

Why did it tickle her that he picked up the subtly of what she'd said? "Uh, not really. That was a point of contention between us. It felt like they saw me as an accessory upgrade. As if I improved his image, thereby, improving theirs."

He leaned forward. "Could that be why he was so desperate to keep you?"

Her shoulders rounded as she nodded. She'd hated feeling like that too, like she had nothing more to give than upping his approval rating to his parents and their sphere of influence. "I think so. For once he had his parent's approval, and he wanted to keep it."

"Meesha, I really don't think you should go on this cruise. This is much more than a guy unwilling to let go. You fulfilled something beyond being a girlfriend," her sister said.

With a sigh, Meesha hugged herself. "I know you don't, but there's no proof he's in the states. I'm not cancelling my trip because he *might* be here. I worked too hard and too long to just cancel it." Plus, there was no way she was letting Glen Hughman go on that trip without her, especially since she was the one paying his way.

Her phone buzzed in her pocket, and she discreetly pulled it out. Speak of the devil. It was the first time she was relieved to see his name pop up.

Glen: Hey, I'm not going to be able to go on the trip.

Forcing herself to keep her composure, she quickly swept her gaze around the people sitting at the table and scooted down a little in her chair to reply. *What do you mean you can't go?*

Glen: I got arrested for public intoxication last night. I just got out on bail, and I've got a hearing in a week.

Working to keep her temper in cheek and her emotions off her face, she returned the text. *Are you serious? After all the money I spent?*

Glen: *I know, and I'm sorry. Things just got out of hand. It's my third offense so they aren't being all that great to me.*

His only saving grace was that he wasn't standing in front of her. The nerve of him. After all the money she'd spent just so he could go. *Please hear me when I say this. I never want to speak to you again. Don't call me, text me, and if you see me and value your life, you should walk the other way.* She blocked his number, deleted it, and shoved her phone back in her pocket.

First Noel. Now Glen. What was wrong with her? She hadn't even expected much from Glen. She'd known he was a loser from the get-go, but with the promise of an all-expense paid vacation, she thought he could keep it together at least long enough to take the trip. She wasn't even worth his loyalty even with the bonus of a tropical getaway.

As angry with him as she was, she was even angrier with herself. Why had she lied in the first place? It'd caused her more problems than she needed. So, what if she didn't have a boyfriend. Was that a crime? No, but she'd snapped the last time Anna gushed about her boyfriend, and now, she didn't feel like she had a way out. Well, other than saying they broke up, but that seemed worse than not having one. That'd mean she couldn't keep a man, or worse, that a man didn't want her.

Kayleigh bumped her arm. "Are you listening?"

Meesha pushed her thoughts aside. No. "Yes."

"Mia and Ryder can't find him," she said, her eyebrows furrowed. "You can't go if they don't know where he is."

Her lips pinched together. All she wanted to do was cry. She felt like she was back in Paris, packing up her apartment, and giving up everything she'd worked for. While this cruise wasn't the equivalent of a life-long career achievement being crushed, it was still something she'd worked for. Meesha shoved out of the chair. "I'm going on that cruise."

"No, you aren't." Kayleigh crossed her arms over her chest as she came out of her chair. "I'm calling Mom and Dad and there is no way they'll let you go either."

Meesha leveled her eyes at Kayleigh. "Then you better be prepared to tie me down, kicking and screaming because that's the only way I'm not going." She spun on her heels, marched to the door, and slammed it as she stormed out.

It was illogical. Completely and totally, but she didn't care. There was no way she was giving Noel one more micro-second of her life. What if they never found him? Was she supposed to spend the rest of her life hiding? No way was she doing that. This cruise was supposed to let her relax, find her groove, and maybe come back ready to put herself back out there. She wasn't cancelling. She just wasn't doing it, and no one was going to make her do it.

4

That'd gone better than Sawyer expected. He'd expected next level screaming and thrown objects. A little sparring and a slammed door were nothing. Honestly, compared to his childhood, it was less than tame.

Groaning, Kayleigh hung her head. "Give me a second, and I'll go talk to her."

"Uh, I don't have a dog in this fight, so maybe I could go talk to her," Sawyer said. "Maybe a neutral party can help."

Tru stood, used one arm to pull Kayleigh close, and tipped her chin up with the tip of his finger. "He's right. She's furious, you're furious, and I'm biased. Maybe she'll listen to him."

With a tiny nod, Kayleigh wrapped her arms around Tru. "Okay."

Pushing out of the chair, Sawyer smiled. "I'll see what I can do. One way or another, we'll keep her safe. You have my word on that."

"Thank you."

Crossing the room, he slipped out the door, and followed the faint sound of crying coming from one of the bedrooms they used when clients needed to stay overnight. He stopped at the door and paused a moment as he watched Meesha, sitting on the edge of the bed, muttering to herself as she swiped tears off her face with her hands.

He softly rapped his knuckles against the door. "Hey, are you okay?"

She jumped and palmed the spot over her heart. "Oh, my goodness." She glanced at him and then waved him off. "I'm fine."

"Well, you don't sound all that fine to me."

With a heavy sigh, she shook her head. "It's okay." She lifted her head but didn't quite meet his gaze. "I'm sure you don't want to hear me whine."

He smiled. "You'd be surprised the things I like to hear."

Her lips quirked up a fraction. With a shrug, she cast her gaze to the floor. Just as he thought she wouldn't respond, she groaned and said, "This cruise has been nothing but a headache. First, getting everyone together on a date and a destination. Then planning all the events and excursions during the cruise. Working with Anna Mears was just as bad this past year as it was in high school. Every club or committee I joined, she joined. Even track and field. It was like she got pleasure from seeing me take second place. Every zoom call felt like I was back in high school."

With a whistle, he stuffed his hands in his pockets. "Can't say that sounds pleasant at all."

"Right?" She choked out a half sob half laugh. "I've just got my life back together, and here Noel comes, waltzing in and taking everything again. Kayleigh's breathing down my neck, telling me I can't go and threatening to tell our parents. He took my job, my freedom, my self-esteem. My confidence. I'm always afraid someone is going to break into my apartment. I have a near panic attack when I find out I have to drive at night."

That didn't surprise him. Most abuse victims suffered the effects of the relationship long after it was over. The abuser either got away with it or served very little jail time. It was never going to be fair in Sawyer's eyes.

She kept her head bowed, but he caught the little jaw movement like she was trying to swallow back more tears. "Want to know what's really pathetic?" She sniffed and used both hands to wipe her cheeks. "I lied about having a boyfriend. Anna was talking about her perfect life and her perfect boyfriend, and I blurted out I had one." Her eyebrows knitted together as she bit her lip.

"I basically hired a guy to go as my date, and he just called and cancelled. Public intoxication. Two days before we leave for a cruise, he gets himself arrested for public intoxication." She huffed, rolling her eyes. "I paid for his flight to Miami and the cruise."

This gorgeous woman with the incredible smile paid a man to go with her? Just how dumb was he? Sawyer would have paid double just to carry her luggage to the boat.

She shook her head. "I know how to pick 'em right? First Noel, and now this guy. What's wrong with me?"

Oh, he couldn't let her think that. He crossed the room and squatted in front of her. "There's nothing wrong with you. Noel is a jerk, and that guy that bailed on you is an idiot."

"I'm just not so sure I believe that anymore," she said through soft sobs.

The promise he'd made to protect her seemed to take root in his bones. It went beyond keeping her physically safe. He wanted to pull her to him, wrap his arms around her, and use himself as a shield to keep her from ever again feeling like she was less than worthy of the best.

Danger blared in his ears, but before his brain could send the warning to his mouth, his heart hijacked him. "I'm not trying to impose on you or anything, but I'm very single and I don't get seasick. A cruise to the Caribbean sounds fantastic to me." The words tumbled out of his mouth like it was being moved by an unseen force.

Her eyebrows knitted together. "What?"

He smiled. "If you'll have me, I'll go with you."

Her perfect lips parted, quirking up at the sides. "You'd do that for me?"

"I sure will." A cruise with her? He'd made a fool of himself in the conference room within five seconds of meeting her? What would he look like at the end of a cruise? He could almost see her patting his head as he wagged his tail, waiting for a *good boy*.

Holding his gaze, her eyebrows and her lips pressed together in a thin line. "That's sweet, but I can't ask you to do that."

It was his escape. His way out. He could be charming enough to keep her off that ship. Sure, he'd promised to keep her safe, but not like that. This went beyond protection. Again, his heart and mouth conspired against him. "You're not. I'm offering. Besides, I promised Tru that I'd keep you safe. Can't do that if I'm here and you're not." He smiled.

She caught her bottom lip in her teeth. "I don't

know. I mean, it's ten days. What if...what if you realize I'm not all that great."

Not all that great? For some strange reason, that just didn't strike him as a possibility. He grinned. "Do you snore?"

She gave him a small smile. "Not that I'm aware of. Do you?"

Shaking his head, he replied, "As far as I know, I don't. I don't hog the hot water either. Do you?"

Her lips curved up a little more and she gave a one shouldered shrug with a cute little giggle at the end. "Honestly? Sometimes."

Talk about cute. He pretended to ponder it for a second. "That's a strike but the honesty makes it even."

"Are you sure? It's not a logical leap to guess you were asked to protect me, and while this is above and beyond kind, I don't want to make things difficult for you? I mean, it's my fault I'm in this mess."

This time, his ducks were marching right in line. How could he look at that sweet face and not go? "You aren't making anything difficult for me. No one will even have to know about the loser who backed out on you. After a brief spat and a stand-off, you reluctantly agreed to tolerate me. We'll even tell them it was my idea."

Meesha's face lit up, and her smile was like basking in the sun. Her eyes twinkled and she laughed. It was light, sweet, musical, and he could listen to it all day long. "Thank you."

He stood and held his hand out to her. Instead of taking his hand, she pushed off the bed and wrapped her arms around his neck tighter than anyone ever had, and whispered, "Thank you."

That wasn't the response he'd been expecting. Even less expected, he was returning it. He didn't mind getting hugs but returning them was a rare event, and he'd done it without so much as a second thought. He took a deep breath, a mix of honey and fruit swirled around him, making him dizzy. He'd made two mistakes in quick succession. He knew his typical lined-up ducks were drunk and looking at him from the back of a police car, when the realization hit that not only did he not mind, but he also enjoyed it.

Leaning back, her smile was nearly blinding and the most beautiful yet.. "You don't know how much this means to me."

He was toast. Black, burnt, can't-scrape-off-to-make-it-edible toast. His head was throwing a full-on tantrum while his heart sighed. What was a little charring if it meant he'd get to see that smile again? "I think I'm getting the better end of the deal."

A blanket of soft pink covered her cheeks as she lowered her gaze. When she looked back up, she was looking at him through a fringe of lashes. His heart hit the stratosphere. She was sexy without even trying. "You're very sweet. I'll never be able to repay you."

Sawyer was pretty sure he was the one who'd never be able to repay her. He'd been given the chance to sail the high seas with a woman who stir-fried his brain in all the best ways possible. His pulse was roaring in his ears, his heart beating at the speed of sound, and his nerves were on fire.

Then he realized why. He was still holding her, and worse, he didn't want to let go. Her curves fit against him so well it was like he'd found his missing piece. Yeah, he was at the end of the plank with his hands bound. He nodded to the door, forcing himself to put a little distance between them. "Why don't we go back to the conference room and see if we can get them on board?"

She gave a quick nod. "Okay."

When they reached the door, he pushed it open, and waved for her to lead. Everyone turned in their direction, but Sawyer kept his head down, still not wanting to chance looking anyone in the eye.

"So, did you guys talk?" asked Kayleigh.

He'd gone in search of her to talk her out of the trip, and he was returning having agreed to go on the cruise with her. His tombstone was going to be inscribed with a picture of a sucker on it.

"We think we've found a reasonable compromise,"

Sawyer said. "That is, if Ryder and Mia can make it happen."

Kayleigh swept her gaze from Sawyer to Meesha. "What's the idea."

"It wasn't easy, but I think we've come to a compromise that will give everyone what they want. I've offered to go on the trip with her—"

"This man tried to hurt her. What if they get on some island and he's waiting for her?" Kayleigh shot out of the chair and walked to them. "Don't you see how dangerous this is? I trust Sawyer, but…he'll have no backup. Nothing."

"We've even run facial recognition on every passenger booked. There's nothing," Ryder said. "I'll continue running it until the ship leaves port, and each time the ship makes a stop."

Mia nodded. "You can take a satellite phone. If something happens, we can reach you or vice versa."

Noah took a deep breath. "It's actually not that bad of an idea. You'll need to stay in the same room. At the very least, connected rooms in case anything happens."

"Got it," Mia said. "Wow, this is one fancy boat. Looks like they had a cancellation. This is a great room. It requires keycard to access the area where the rooms are located, it has a private balcony, and two rooms with two bathrooms."

Noah shook his head. "It's Meesha's decision. If she's okay—"

"I just..." Kayleigh looked from Sawyer to Meesha. "If..."

"Kayleigh," Sawyer said. "I'll keep her safe. If at any point I get a weird feeling or think anything is off, I'll call in. I won't let anything happen to her. I promise."

Just then, Tru stood, crossed the room, and hugged her from behind. "Sweetheart, I love her too, but we need to let her make the decision."

Kayleigh turned in his arms, her bottom lip trembling. "But..."

Meesha sagged. "I know you're worried. I completely get it, but not going means he wins. Again..." Her voice broke. "I can't let him have this."

"Honey, she needs this." Tru took Kayleigh's face in his hands, touching his lips to her forehead. "While she's on the cruise, we'll focus on this creep, and find him."

Kayleigh sighed and used her shirt sleeve to wipe her eyes. "All right. I guess if that's the decision, then we need to get you to Myrtle Beach so you can get packed."

Meesha exhaled and smiled. "Thank you," she said, and bear hugged her, swaying side to side.

Noah nodded to Sawyer. "Go get packed and we'll meet you at the plane."

"I won't take long," Sawyer said and strode out of the room.

Oh, he was in trouble. Heaps and heaps of trouble. And it was all his own fault. He'd gone from talking her out of the trip to not only going but going as her fake boyfriend. He'd given his word to Tru, Kayleigh, and Meesha, though, and he'd keep it. It was ten days and he was overreacting. By the time they reached Miami, his head would be clear, his heart would be on the same page, and at the end of those ten days, he'd be an island unto himself. Easy peasy, his head barked as his heart sighed and wished him the best of luck.

5

The flight to Myrtle Beach was so quick, Meesha felt like she'd blinked and Sawyer was escorting her to her apartment so she could finish packing. It'd taken a little longer because she'd changed her mind about a few outfits. Not that she expected anything to happen between them, she just wanted to look… better. Besides, he was a professional. He probably did things like this all the time. Well, maybe not the fake boyfriend part, but traveling with women he was guarding.

Now cruising at thirty-thousand-feet on their way to Miami, she was still pinching herself that he'd offered to not only go with her on the cruise, but he was going to pretend to be her boyfriend. It'd further convinced her that she was right about him passing his measurement with flying colors.

As she watched Sawyer sitting across from her with his head turned toward the window, she was hopeful that maybe she could find a way to show him how thankful she was that he'd come with her. She hadn't looked forward to spending time with Glen. Sure, she thought he was attractive, but the air between his ears was a drawback. Her gut told her there was way more depth to Sawyer.

He'd been so quiet since they left Guardian Group headquarters, she wondered if he was having second thoughts. Maybe in the heat of the moment, he'd felt sorry for her and rushed in without thinking it through.

"If you're having second thoughts, it's okay to back out," Meesha said.

He rolled his head, a smile quirking on his lips. "No way. I'm looking forward to it."

"You're just really quiet, and as much as I appreciate it, I don't want you to feel sorry for me."

"No, I don't feel sorry for you. This whole thing worked out in my favor. First, I get to spend ten days with you, and second, I get to take a cruise. It's a win-win."

That helped quell some of the worry. Still, she hoped it'd be a good trip. "I think it'll be fun. We've got some pretty cool stuff planned. A scavenger hunt, snorkeling in St. Thomas, and a few other things. Well, you already knew that."

He shot her a half-smile. "I don't think I'll need all that to enjoy the trip."

Her cheeks heated. "You know you're charming, right?"

"Doesn't make it any less true." He chuckled.

Shaking her head, she took a deep breath. Her face was going to burst into flames if he kept this up. A change of subject was needed. They *were* going to pretend to be dating. Maybe getting to know one another would make it easier. At the same time, he was doing her a favor. She didn't want to come off as prying. "Would it be okay if I asked you a few questions? Just in case someone asks?"

He held her gaze for a moment, like he was battling himself for the answer. "Sure."

"How did you find Guardian Group?" she asked in the hopes it'd be innocent enough that maybe she could start gaining his trust. Maybe he could use a friend as much as she did.

The sigh he gave was nearly too soft to hear. "A guy named Kolby Rutherford. He worked for them before he met his wife, Ivy. She was on a multi-author book tour, and I was providing protection for one of the other authors. We struck up a conversation and became pretty good friends. I didn't like my employer. A few weeks later, Noah approached me about working for him."

"Tru and Kayleigh love working there. I've only met Noah and the rest of the team a few times, but they all seem like good people."

He nodded. "They are, and they've been good to me. Noah is a good man to work for, and I call all of them friends."

Her gaze dipped to his bare feet. "Have you always liked to go barefoot?"

"My family was poor when I was growing up. I only got new shoes when we found them cheap enough at the thrift store or when people gave them to us, so my shoes rarely ever fit, and more often than not, they were too small. I can't stand the feeling of them. I only wear them when I have no other choice. That's one of the reasons I like Noah. He doesn't care as long as I don't get myself injured."

She leaned her head against the back of her seat. "I had a student like that. She hated shoes. The headmaster, the parents, and I worked together to develop a way to encourage her to keep her shoes on. We began having instruction in the morning, and once that was done, we'd go to recess until the end of the school day. I won my two-year contract because it worked so well. Students were outperforming other classes of the same age and the headmaster and parents were thrilled."

His face lit up. "That's great. I bet the kids loved it."

"They did. We spent more time outside than inside during the spring term. Weather could be a challenge sometimes, especially in the winter, but with the help of my headmaster, I took an old, unused classroom and turned into an indoor playground."

Tilting his head, Sawyer grinned. "Oh, they didn't just love you, they adored you."

The words were like a stab in the heart. They had, and she'd loved them equally as much. "It was mutual."

"Did you miss your family while you were living over there?"

"I did, but we called, texted, video chatted as a family. We worked hard to keep in touch. I'd planned to visit when school was on break, but..." She rubbed the spot over her heart. It'd been three years, and yet the sting felt fresh.

He winced. "I'm sorry. I wasn't thinking. I shouldn't have asked."

She shrugged. "It's okay. Well, not okay, but it's done now. I'm happy in Myrtle Beach." As much as she could be. "What about you? Do you have family you keep in touch with?"

Shaking his head, he said, "No, I had a pretty rough upbringing. My parents were drug addicts and neglectful. They'd run through money, and there'd be nothing left for food or clothes. We were homeless more than once. After I left for the Army, they got clean, and we were reconciling when they were killed in a home invasion by a drug dealer who felt slighted by them for going clean."

Her mouth dropped open. She couldn't imagine that level of pain. She loved her family, even when Kayleigh was being overbearing, Meesha knew it was out of love. "That's…horrible. Now, I wish I hadn't asked. I'm so sorry." As awful as that sounded, she had a feeling his childhood had nothing to do with his comment about measuring up.

"You're fine." He paused. "I won't lie, it was a hit to the heart, but I was glad I'd agreed to reconcile. Talking to them, working some of the things out that happened when I was a kid, helped me. It would have hurt worse if we hadn't worked on our relationship."

She didn't know how to respond. What words were there? He'd lost his parents, and she had no idea how to relate to that sort of pain. Sure, her relationship with Noel had caused her loss, but not her family. If she hadn't had them to help her weather that storm, there was no telling where she'd have landed.

Silence stretched out as she searched for something to talk about. She looked at her hands in her lap. "I guess if anyone asks how we met, we can go the simple route and say we met through my sister and her husband." She exhaled heavily. "Or I could just be an adult and come clean about lying." The thought made her sick, but maybe that was better. Of course, Anna would rub it in her nose like always. What was one more "L" stamped on her forehead?

"Are you trying to get rid of me?" he asked with a chuckle.

"No," she said softly.

Air moved around her and when she looked up, Sawyer was sitting next to her. "Hey, everything's okay. While you were packing, it dawned on me that maybe this was a great idea. Ryder and Mia are excellent at what they do, but they can't beat a human being. What if the facial recognition scan fails and Noel slips through?"

That hadn't even crossed her mind. What if he did get past their technology and what would he do to her if he got to her this time? She was alive because of a neighbor. Alone. On a cruise. A shiver ran down her spine. "You think he could?"

Sawyer shrugged. "I don't, but I do know his type. There's no way he'll be able to stay hidden if he thinks we're together."

"I guess you have a point." A great point really. "He hated it anytime a man looked my way or vice versa. We were at a dinner with his parents one night, and a man looked at me. I guess Noel thought we made eye contact a little too long, and he was awful."

It'd been the first night Noel put his hands on her, and the pivotal moment in their relationship that made her question why she'd stayed with him. Not only had he hurt her, but he'd also threatened—she sucked in a sharp breath. Sawyer. "We can't do this. That night he threatened the man who looked at me. I'd never be able to live with myself if something happened to you all because I was being petulant and pigheaded."

He shot her a heart-jolting half smile oozing confidence. "I don't need a weapon to take him down. It'd make things easier for sure, but I have a black belt in Brazilian Jui-Jitsu."

She chewed her bottom lip as her eyebrows knitted together. "I don't know."

"If you think about it, this actually works better. You won't be lying to Anna. You'll be working undercover with Guardian Group to catch a man who's violated a flight ban."

Well, that certainly gave her a better motive than lying to impress Anna, and Meesha liked that a whole lot more. "Okay, I guess that *does* work better. I mean, if Noel manages to get on the ship, pretending we're dating will absolutely draw him out."

"Exactly." He grinned wider. "And, I was honest when I said I've never been to the Caribbean, and now that I know I'll get to go snorkeling, it's even better. That's two bucket list items in one shot. On top of all that, I'll get to check them off with a beautiful woman next to me."

She bumped his shoulder with hers. He'd rescued her from spiraling into a funk, and he'd done it with sound logic instead of superficial flattery. "Thank you."

"I think this will be a great trip, and I'm not just saying that."

If nothing else, this trip would be fun because he was with her. While she didn't know him very well, so far she liked him, and she had a feeling he'd be an easy man to fall for. His charm and kind heart were a serious draw.

Meesha waved the thought away. He was her bodyguard, and he was there to protect her. Nothing else. He was only being nice because he'd promised her sister he'd keep her safe. That's all. There'd be no falling. She'd return from the trip as single as she was currently.

6

Sawyer spent the last half of the trip to Miami making a bullet point list of rules he'd use while on the cruise. He'd watched the storm clouds roll over Meesha, and his heart and mouth had plotted against him. She was giving him an out, and before he knew it, he was switching seats, persuading her to work with him to catch Noel. It'd been nobler than just wanting to spend time with her too.

What was it about this woman? She'd set a hook in his mouth, and every time she'd tried to pull it out, he'd clamped down harder on it. Plenty of women had tried throwing their line in his pond, and he'd swiftly shown them the road. Not Meesha though. He liked seeing her smile, and he liked it even more when he knew he was the source of it.

By the time they'd landed, he'd regained his

composure and his professionalism. Well, as much as he could. Every time she looked at him, it felt like all his reasons were built on sand and a tornado was bearing down on them.

They'd started the check-in process prior to landing in Miami which made finishing the process quicker when they arrived at port. Just before they boarded, Sawyer had called Ryder to get the all-clear. According to him, facial recognition scans had still found nothing. He'd be calling Ryder again the day after tomorrow once they reached Jamaica.

Once that was done, they made the trek to the rooms. Overall, he was impressed with the entire ship. There were crew members everywhere, offering directions or whatever else a guest might need, and with the three thousand plus people on board, it still felt wide and open.

While she'd packed, Ryder sent Sawyer the ship's layout and their room. The area where they would stay was called The Getaway—a rear portion of the ship comprised of three decks with exclusive restaurants, pools, and private elevators that required keycards for access.

They'd each have their own king size bed and bathroom with common areas to share, like the living room, dining area, and balcony where they had access to a private balcony with a hot tub. He was especially grateful for the separate bathrooms. He was already struggling when it came to Meesha, so he didn't need any bathing-towel mishaps.

Sawyer used the cabin keycard, stepped inside, then held the door for her. A wall of windows lined the far side of the cabin, allowing a view of the balcony and ocean. "Wow."

"Yeah, this room is way nicer than what I'd booked. All I could afford was an interior cabin, so I was expecting something claustrophobic," Meesha said, looking around as she followed him inside with her carry-on luggage in tow. "This is better than my apartment."

He swept his gaze from one side of the room to the other. "Definitely bigger than my room at Guardian Group." The view was definitely better. Seeing the open ocean every morning for the next ten days would be a treat.

"You live at Guardian Group?" she asked.

He shrugged. "Yeah, but I like it. I'm available when they need me."

"Makes the commute to work a lot easier." She grinned.

He chuckled. "That is one of the perks." It also meant he didn't have to sit in an apartment all by himself either.

"Let me check the cabin, and I'll be right back," he said, dropping his duffle bag next to her luggage.

Out of habit, he reached for his service weapon before entering the bedroom to the right and remembered he didn't have it. No weapons were allowed on board. They did have security, as well as vaults with weapons should they need them, but that was only accessible by ship security guards. Without any weapons on his person, he'd be leaning on all those years of learning Brazilian jiu-jitsu.

As far as cabins went, the layout made it feel open and spacious. The private balcony was a cool feature, but it was also a weak point. Once he did a thorough check, he returned to Meesha. "All clear." He scanned the room again. "Everything seems so new, it's almost like it was just built."

"Because it was. That was one of the reasons I fought so hard for this specific cruise. This is only its third voyage." She looked down at his feet. "Are you going barefoot while we're here?"

"No, I'm on duty."

"Oh, right. I guess you are." Her lips turned down for a fraction of a second, and just as fast, they quirked back up. "I was going to tell you that I didn't care either way, but it might not be wise for sanitary reasons. I know this is only the third voyage, but..." She grimaced.

"People are gross?" He laughed.

"Yeah and mix a little alcohol in there and you've got a whole thing going on that you don't want to walk through barefoot."

Chuckling, Sawyer threw a thumb over his shoulder. "The rooms are equally spaced in relation to the balcony and the entrance as far as security goes, so which is your pick?"

She smiled. "Either is fine."

He grabbed her luggage, and she followed him to the bedroom. When he reached the bed he set it on top. "Were you wanting to stay here a while or…?"

Pulling her phone from her pocket, she checked the time. "We've got about two hours before the group meets tonight. Since I'm on the planning committee, I need to be there earlier than the rest of them, so I was thinking I'd get ready for it."

"All right." He looked down at himself. When he'd thrown on the shirt and jeans that morning he'd had no idea he'd end the day on a cruise. "Is what I'm wearing okay?"

She nodded. "Tonight's casual so you're fine. I'm the one who threw on clothes in a hurry to get to Greenville this morning."

This was how she looked when she'd just thrown something on? Before his imagination could get the better of him, he shut it down. Client. Friend's sister. "Okay, see you in a few."

A smile and a nod answered him as she shut the door to her room.

He grabbed his bag as he crossed the cabin to his room, and paused as he caught his reflection in the mirror. She'd said he was fine, but he looked more than a little rough. He *was* playing the part of her boyfriend, and if he was dating her, he wouldn't show up for a date looking like a hungover frat boy.

Once he'd picked out a decent pair of jeans and a polo shirt, he trimmed the scruff lining his jaw and lip, quickly showered, and dressed. Whether she'd planned it or not, she'd given them a room where the balcony faced the sea. He stepped out onto the balcony and walked the length of it before settling himself where Meesha could see him when she was finished getting ready.

As far as assignments went, this one was in his top five. While he'd taken his shower, the ship had set sail and Miami was fading by the second. It was already infinitely more peaceful and relaxing. Out in the open sea, it'd be even better. Maybe he'd sleep outside to take advantage of it. Taking a deep breath, he let the salty air fill his nose and lungs as he closed his eyes. When he retired, he was going to find himself a secluded spot on an island and sleep outside every chance he got.

Footsteps caught his attention, and he turned just as Meesha walked onto the balcony. "You didn't need to change."

His jaw dropped. Man, was she something. She'd looked great before, but now he felt underdressed. The strapless, pale-yellow dress complemented her skin tone and showed off her soft-looking shoulders and delicate collarbone. She'd pulled her hair up, leaving little pieces framing her nearly makeup free face with shiny lip gloss that made her lips a million times more kissable than they were a few hours ago. A thought he shouldn't even have.

"You look incredible." He smiled. "Just wow."

A blanket of pink covered her cheeks as her lips curved up higher. "Thank you."

The want to kiss her only seemed to grow each time he saw her. If he was going to survive ten days, they'd be spending the majority of their time anywhere but the cabin. He held out his arm. "Ready to go?"

She slipped her arm through his, nodding. "Yep."

They walked through the cabin out the front door and strolled down the hallway, passing other passengers with luggage headed in the opposite direction. When they reached the elevator, she faced him, and stepped a little closer, straightening the collar of his polo. "You really didn't have to change." She drew her thumb across the corner of his mouth and held up a piece of hair. "You didn't have to shave either."

Being near her was hard enough, and with her this close, looking and smelling so great, his pulse was hitting a level that made him dizzy. He swallowed hard. "I just thought if we were dating, I wouldn't go out looking like I'd rolled out of bed."

"Well, you look great." She palmed his chest. "I like your cologne too." Her eyes met his making his heart thrum in his ears.

This woman was off-limits in a multitude of ways, and for the life of him, at that moment, he couldn't recall even one. With his mind so muddled, he was sure he was hallucinating because he could actually hear a choir of little Jamaican voices telling him to kiss the girl. Where was that elevator?

"Don't freak okay?" Her voice was low and sexy.

He needed that elevator pronto. "Uh, okay."

A second later, her lips brushed across his and she leaned back. "It occurred to me that we may have to kiss, and it'd be better if it didn't feel awkward."

His head bobbed like it was attached to his neck by a spring. "We do need to make it look good if we want to catch Noel." Whether he was saying that to himself or her, he had no idea.

"Absolutely."

He slipped one arm around her back, pulled her flush to him, and cupped her cheek before touching his lips to hers. Nothing could have prepared him for the fireworks popping behind his eyes. Her lips were softer than he could have imagined, and he was positive he could taste blackberries.

The feathery kisses continued until she caught his bottom lip in her teeth and a low moan came from deep in his throat. It was music, and he knew right then and there, he was done. Her lips parted and just as he went to deepen the kiss, the elevator dinged. Before the doors could open fully, they jumped apart as their momentary bubble burst.

For such a small kiss, Sawyer felt clobbered. He nodded to the two couples already occupying the elevator as he and Meesha got on. She punched the number seven and tucked a piece of hair behind her ear.

Whew, was that a great kiss. If that tiny kiss had his head swimming what would a real kiss do to him? There'd be no more kissing her, not if he wanted even a sporting chance of having a somewhat intact heart by the time this cruise was over.

Meesha leaned in, setting her mouth next to his ear. "I only did that just in case anyone was watching us. Okay? I just wanted to make sure our relationship looked real."

"I know. We're good." Good? More like eternally wrecked. "It was smart thinking." He smiled.

"Yeah," she said softly. If he didn't know any better, she sounded like she was disappointed, but when she leaned back, he saw nothing in her features that indicated it.

He pushed the thought away. Meesha was out of his league to begin with, and once she learned that he'd killed someone, she'd never look at him the same way again. He just needed to make it ten days, and he'd handled worse things for longer than that. All he needed to do was remember this pep talk when he was close to her. If that was possible.

So far, nearness to her was like kryptonite, and he had a sinking suspicion it'd get harder to resist her the longer he was around her, especially now that he knew he'd be dreaming about those lips of hers and that sensational kiss. He could dream all he wanted, and that's where it stopped. Yeah, ten days were a drop in the bucket.

7

Meesha still felt dizzy. That all-too-brief, sizzling kiss with Sawyer was a game changer. From this point forward, she'd be comparing future kisses with an impossible standard.

He looked incredible and smelled even better. It'd taken a She-Ra level of restraint to keep herself from leaning over and breathing him in. When they'd reached the elevator, all she'd meant to do was straighten his collar a little, and nothing else. One second, she was standing there, and the next, wham, she was brushing her lips across his. She'd expected him to set her straight, instead he'd pulled her against his hard body, cupped her cheek, and she was in heaven. His lips were even softer than she could imagine, and her knees were wobbly just thinking about it.

She'd seen the look of horror on his face when they got on the elevator and quickly came up with a reason for kissing him. For a second, she'd been disappointed, but she'd stuffed that silly emotion down. He was doing her a favor by accompanying her on the cruise, and he was a trained professional. Of course, he would have known what she was doing and played along.

"Thank you for helping me get setup." Meesha said, finishing the last table centerpiece. Sweeping her gaze from one end to the other, she was pleased with how great it looked. Hopefully, the thirty classmates plus their families or plus-ones attending would agree. All the photos…sheesh, they'd all been so young, and the ten years had flown by so quickly.

"You did a great job," Sawyer said as he stopped next to her. He'd stepped in to help when she'd realized Anna was up to her old tricks, leaving Meesha to do the dirty work and then taking all the credit.

"Thanks, and thanks for helping me."

He waved her off. "Eh, you could have done it without me."

"Maybe." She worked to infuse her voice with enthusiasm. It didn't reach her heart though. Each time she talked with a classmate or received an email, her shortcomings were so visible. With a deep breath, she forced the thoughts down. Tonight was about catching up and having fun, not silly jealousy. "But I'm still thankful for the help." She smiled.

"Meesha!" That voice. Meesha sucked in a deep breath, turned, and faced Anna Mears who'd arrived in typical flamboyant fashion with her boyfriend in tow. In white ankle pants and a soft pink blouse that showed off one of her shoulders. Her blond hair was down and brushed the tops of her shoulders.

Suddenly, all the confidence Meesha felt just moments ago, was gone.

"It's so good to see you," Anna said, embracing Meesha.

"Hey Anna, it's good to see you too." She limply hugged her back.

Anna leaned back, smiling. "I'm so sorry I'm late." Stepping back, she hugged her boyfriend's arm. "We went exploring and lost track of time."

Of course, she did. Some things never changed. She was always late, and still managed to beat Meesha at everything. Just as well, at least she didn't have to deal with Anna harping on how she was doing it wrong.

"It's okay," Meesha said and bumped Sawyer's shoulder. "He helped so it wasn't too bad. Anna, this is my boyfriend."

"Sawyer James. It's nice to meet you," he said, shaking hands with Anna.

Anna shook his hand. "It's nice to meet you, too. This is my boyfriend, Tim Parsons."

Tim shook Sawyer's hand. "Nice to meet you."

The man turned his attention to Meesha and held her gaze with an unnerving stare. "Nice to meet you."

The second her hand touched his, a shiver ran down her spine. What an odd feeling. She'd never seen the man before in her life. Most likely, it was her irritation with Anna that had rubbed off on her innocent boyfriend. High school Meesha needed to grow up. She smiled, ignoring the weird vibe she got from him. "It's nice to meet you too."

Anna pulled away from Tim and walked to the table. "This looks great." She picked up one of the photos. "Daniel Garcia and Trip Davis. Those two were a hoot, weren't they?" She moved along the table and picked up another photo, gasping. "Hannah Easley," Anna pirouetted on her toes, holding up the framed photo. "Did you ever see her becoming a model?"

Really? Was Anna that self-absorbed that she didn't realize Hannah was a model? "Actually, yeah. She was modeling in high school. That's why she was absent so much."

Her mouth dropped open. "How did I miss that?"

Meesha wanted to reply with *Your ginormous ego*, but instead opted for something safer. "We were all working on our own stuff. It was easy to miss things."

"That's so true." Anna faced Meesha. "I know I was so busy with all the clubs and stuff. Senior year was the worst of all. Having to go to nationals for the debate club and track, the mock trial championship…" She gave a big sigh and tilted her head. "Didn't you go to the championship?"

Meesha shook her head. "No, I didn't."

"Oh, that's right. We tied for debate club, and I won the run-off." Anna lifted onto her toes and waved. "Terry! I just have to say hello to her." She snagged Tim's hand as she went to greet another classmate.

"Right." The word came out soft. Man, she was pathetic. It was high school for crying out loud. She wasn't even the same person anymore.

Sawyer moved a little closer. "Are you okay?"

"Oh, yeah, I'm fine." She palmed his chest, not quite meeting his eyes. "Thank you for all you've done."

He set one finger under her chin and lifted her head until their eyes met. "Are you okay?"

What did she say? Nothing. She was wallowing like a pro. It'd been ten years, and she needed to build a bridge and take a flamethrower to it the second she was firmly on the other side. Nodding, she gave him her best grin. "Yeah, I am. She just gets under my skin sometimes."

"All right. You let me know if you aren't. I'm here

to keep you safe. That means all of you." His lips lifted in a warm smile.

"Thank you."

More of her classmates filtered in, and from there it was two hours of small talk, catching up on each other's lives—leaving out the part about Paris because it was a rabbit hole Meesha didn't want to fall into nor did she want to see the pity in anyone's eyes. It was bad enough coming from her friends and family.

Mostly, everyone seemed to have a great life. Of course, not everything was roses and cupcakes, but they all seemed happy and content with their careers and families. By the time dinner was over and the centerpieces were put away, Meesha felt like she'd lived a week in one day.

As they walked off the elevator, she kept her gaze pinned to the floor as her thoughts swirled like a tornado. It wasn't until she ran into Sawyer's extended arm that she noticed a few couples standing in their doorways talking to cruise employees.

"Stay close," Sawyer said as he led her down the hall to their room, stopping as they reached the door opening of their cabin.

A female cruise employee with a name tag that ready *Diana* met them at the door.

"What's going on?" asked Sawyer. His voice wasn't exactly gruff, but Meesha made a mental note that she didn't want to be on the other end of a conversation if he ever was upset.

"Hi, I'm so sorry. It appears we've had someone break into a few rooms. Our ship's security is currently taking statements from those on this floor who arrived to find their rooms ransacked."

Meesha absentmindedly pressed herself against Sawyer. "Ransacked?" Her stomach dropped. Noel? It wasn't possible. Kayleigh raved about Ryder and Mia. They were the best and if they said Noel wasn't on the ship, then he wasn't. Right?

Diana wrung her hands. "Yes, ma'am. I'd actually come to the floor to introduce myself, and let you know I'd be your concierge for the cruise when I found several doors open with obvious signs that someone had broken in. We're not sure how that happened, but we're in the process of issuing new keycards and we are checking the security footage now. I can't express how sorry I am for all this."

The poor woman. How many passengers were victims and how many of them took it out on her? "It's a big ship. There's bound to be a bad apple. It's not your fault. I'm just glad you're taking measures to fix it."

Sawyer nodded as he looked at Meesha. "We should probably check our things in case anything might be missing."

"Yes, please. If anything's missing, just make a list, and I'll do whatever I can to replace what was taken."

Leading her into the cabin, Sawyer gave her a look and she nodded as she shut the door. He needed to check them himself to make sure their room was secure. Once he'd made a sweep, he returned to her. "Our stuff was dumped out, but I checked mine a little, and didn't notice anything missing."

"Okay," she said, crossing the cabin into her room. She walked to the bed and paused as a piece of jewelry caught her eye. She picked it up, looking it over. It was the first gift Noel had ever given her. She was positive she'd thrown it away before she left Paris, but she'd been so frazzled after he hurt her that it was possible she'd remembered wrong.

Sawyer joined her at the bed. "Did they take anything?"

She rifled through the pile a little more and shook her head. "No, I don't think so." Turning to him, she smiled. "Honestly, I'm so tired, I'm not sure I could give an accurate accounting of what I brought with me."

His gaze roamed over her face as he nodded. "Yeah, you've had a pretty long day. Why don't you get some rest. I'll stay up, wait for the keycards, and check on you in a little bit."

The polite side of her wanted to argue that it wasn't

fair to make him stay up. That he was probably just as tired as she was, but the will to do it just wasn't there. "That sounds like a plan."

"All right, well I'll leave you to that." He crossed the small distance to the door, paused, and said, "I'll see you in the morning."

The door clicked shut, and Meesha eased herself onto the edge of it. The day had kicked her rear end. She felt beaten, run over, and shredded. The fight with her sister, taking Sawyer up on his offer, and then like an idiot, kissing him. She pushed her things aside and curled up on the bed.

When she'd made the plans to take the cruise, she'd told herself that she'd spend the trip working on herself so that when she returned to Myrtle Beach, she could dip her toe into the dating pool again.

Her one-bedroom apartment was great when she first moved into it. Lately though, it'd become a reminder of what was missing in her life. Her teaching position in Myrtle Beach felt more like a second-place prize. On top of that she was lonely. Every time she saw Kayleigh and Tru, it made her ache for what they had. Love, commitment, a future with someone who loved and supported her.

Tonight, she would sleep. Tomorrow, she'd deal with whatever emotional ramifications were from the would-be burglar, if there were any. Maybe she'd take that last piece of jewelry, toss it into the ocean, and consider that her first step to really moving on.

It sure sounded like a plan. It could be the visual representation of what she would being doing mentally. A smile formed on her lips as her eyes slid shut. Tomorrow was a new day, and she'd do whatever it took to be a new Meesha by the end of it.

8

For the second day in a row, Sawyer had used sheer will to drag himself out of bed just as the sun rose. Not that he ever slept well to begin with, but he'd spent the day at sea with Meesha, traipsing all over the ship and selfies at different locations for the scavenger hunt.

That first night, while waiting for new keycards, he'd reported the incident with the cabin to Ryder. They'd concluded that it most likely wasn't Noel since nothing was taken from any of the cabins nor was anything destroyed which didn't fit the typical profile of a stalker.

Currently, he was throwing back his second cup of coffee as Meesha and her fellow reunion-ers and their families or plus ones ate breakfast and chit-chatted as they waited for the last two people in their group to show, Anna and Tim. Once they arrived, they'd be disembarking the ship for Ocho Rios, Jamaica, as a group for a photo, and then breaking up to check out the island.

"Where is she?" Meesha pulled her phone from her pocket and pursed her lips. "Twenty-minutes late. We only have so much time to explore the island."

"Maybe her cabin was broken into as well and she couldn't sleep. I know I'm dragging this morning."

A long sigh poured from her. "True. Just because she was late last night doesn't mean she's pulling the same stunts she was in high school. Maybe she got lost or something and was too embarrassed to own it." She paused, her shoulders rounding. "Guess I need to stop letting the past color my opinion of her."

What a woman. Gorgeous and gracious. If only her well was deep enough to cover his transgressions... He quickly pushed the thoughts away. He wouldn't entertain the possibility. "We're all guilty of that from time to time."

Her lips curved into a smile as she bumped his shoulder. "Thank you." She studied his face a moment before palming his cheek. "I'm sorry you didn't sleep well last night. Our day isn't planned down to the minute. We could do a few of the items on the list, take a break, and you could take a nap."

Where the coffee had failed to wake him up, her

touch succeeded and now he was wide awake. "Aw, I'll be all right."

Her hand dropped to her lap. "Okay, well, if you change your mind, let me know. It won't bother me at all to hole up in the cabin and sit on the balcony a while." Her gaze dipped to the floor. "How are your feet? Are they still okay? I know you said you wear shoes when you're on an assignment, but that doesn't mean they're comfortable."

"They're fine." Well, they were until she brought them to his attention. Now, they were a little less fine. He wouldn't risk an injury though. Plus, he'd had a broken toe once, and was positive he could qualify for a Guiness record for number of times he hit it on a chair.

"All right. I was—"

"I am so sorry for being so late!" Anna's voice carried from the front of the restaurant. With Tim in tow, she weaved through the tables and dropped a stack of papers on the table next to Sawyer. "I was looking over the scavenger hunt and thought it needed a little more excitement, so one of the crew members helped me change a few things and get a new list printed."

"What?" Meesha asked, looking at the stack of papers. "You told us to take care of it because you were going on vacation. We did, and then you went and changed it?"

"It's my cruise too and it needed a little more action. You put snorkeling on there, and nothing else. So, I added bobsledding, swimming with dolphins, and a couple more things."

"Those things are really pricey," Meesha waved her hand at the people at the table. "That's why we only had one big thing on there because not everyone can afford to do all those things."

Anna smiled. "I know." She smiled at Tim. "That's why Tim has offered to pay for the bobsledding and I'm paying for the dolphins. The other things on there are very cheap, even accounting for those with children."

Tim put his arm around Anna's waist. "We really weren't trying to cause trouble."

Terry Hanks shook her head. "I don't know about anyone else, but I sure don't mind. This is going to be the most amazing trip I've ever had."

"See? It's no big deal," Anna said.

Meesha sighed. "You could have at least talked to the committee first."

Anna began passing out the new list and excited chatter grew louder as it reached each person. "I just assumed if the cost was covered, you wouldn't mind."

Sawyer glanced over the list, and he had to admit

that adding the bobsledding and dolphins did add to the fun. He also appreciated Meesha's budget consideration since several of her classmates had children, and things could get exponentially expensive for families.

Pulling his phone from his pocket, he took a picture of the new list and shot it to Ryder. He didn't expect trouble, but it didn't hurt to keep the team informed.

Looking around the table, Meesha nodded. "I guess if there are no objections, then it's fine." A hint of disappointment laced the words.

Tim touched Meesha on the shoulder. "Are you sure? You were responsible for it, weren't you?"

Meesha blinked. "Um, yeah, and it's fine. Really. I was mostly concerned with affordability for everyone. It's very nice of you to do this for us."

The man pinned his attention to Meesha and grinned. "My pleasure."

Sawyer felt uneasy about the way Tim stared at Meesha. The man was smiling. He even seemed genuine, but the vibe was just off, especially when it continued and became so uncomfortable she lowered her gaze to the table.

Anna brightened. "Great. Tim and I ate while we got the new list printed, so we could go when everyone was ready. We should have plenty of time to zipline and do a little shopping and make it back to the ship before it leaves port."

As several people in the group stood, Sawyer leaned over and whispered, "Everything okay?"

Meesha nodded. "Yeah, I'm just surprised."

Sawyer tilted his head. "Did everyone know you were handling the list? You seemed a little surprised that Tim knew."

"I was. We were running out of time, and the committee was like wrangling ducks on speed, so I just did it. When I finally sent it out, I just presented it to everyone as if the whole committee worked on it. I guess Anna told him, which I think was the more surprising news."

"Maybe she has changed then."

Her lips quirked up. "Maybe. If nothing else, I'm willing to give her the benefit of the doubt. It's been ten years, and I know I'm not the same person. I don't want people seeing me the same, and I need to do the same for her."

Oh yeah, she was totally his type. Introspective, and willing to extend mercy. He'd worked with enough clients to appreciate the character that took.

Once everyone was packed up, they headed to the island as a group, stopping next to the welcome sign to take a group photo. Of course, it took a lot of snaps to make sure they got a good one they could post on their social media accounts.

Since the bobsledding wasn't too far from the port of call, they did that first to make sure they had the time they needed for everyone to get a turn. It was a cool place, and getting to the bobsled by sky lift was fun. Then the ride through the forest made the experience even better.

Meesha pushed her hair back as they reached their drop off point which happened to be the pickup point as well. "I don't know about you, but my breakfast is gone."

Now that she mentioned it. "Yeah, I'm thinking something to eat would be good. Maybe we can walk around a little bit after that." He took a deep breath. "I'm thinking this place might test the limits of my self-control."

"Yeah, I know. It's like the wind has a finger and is pulling me by the nose." She laughed.

Like it was a habit, Sawyer tangled his fingers in hers, little zips of electricity shooting up his arm. They seemed to hit every time his skin met hers, and he'd found himself enjoying it more each time it happened. "Let's see what we can find."

"Uh, okay." Her gaze dipped to their fingers. "You don't have to hold my hand," she said looking around. "There's no one here."

He looked around. "Oh, yeah." He pulled his hand free, and for a brief second, thought he saw a flash of disappointment. Maybe his hunger was affecting his mental state.

They wandered around the area a little until they found a small place by the ocean. It boasted jerk chicken and pudding—a local food that they both wanted to try.

"Meesha!" Anna called from a booth on the far side of the dining area. She half stood and waved for them. "Sit with us."

"Fantastic." Meesha smiled and tangled her fingers in Sawyer's as they crossed the room. "Hey, Anna, Tim."

"Is this island amazing or what?" Anna beamed.

"Gorgeous, and the bobsledding was so much fun," Meesha said. "Thank you again for being so generous."

Tim held her gaze as his eyes narrowed a fraction. "You're very welcome. I'm glad I didn't step on any toes."

"Nope, my toes are pain free." She chuckled.

Smiling, Tim maintained eye contact. "Good to know," he said, his voice dipping low, almost like he was flirting and right in front of his girlfriend.

The green-eyed monster reared its ugly head, hitting Sawyer square in the chest. There was something about the guy that didn't sit well with him. He discreetly pulled out his phone and paused a moment before tapping out a text to Ryder, asking him to dig into Tim Parsons.

This had nothing to do with jealousy. The word stopped Sawyer's thoughts in their tracks. His head and heart bickered a minute, and he quickly shut them down. He wasn't jealous. He was doing his job. His heart could stuff it.

9

Meesha leaned into Sawyer as they waited for their food. Having lunch with Anna wasn't her idea of fun, but she wasn't going to be rude, especially when it seemed that Anna was trying to be nice. Plus, Sawyer was right. It was time to stop holding onto grudges.

Tim, on the other hand, she could do without. This was her third interaction with the man, and he was still making her skin crawl with zero justification for it. He'd done nothing but look her in the eyes. Granted, it did seem to have an intensity and last longer than normal, but there were plenty of people like that. Noel would do it as well.

Maybe that's why she felt so uneasy around Tim. He reminded her of Noel. Now that she understood the root cause, she'd make a conscious effort to stop.

The guy had offered to pay for everyone to swim with dolphins which meant he had to be rich too. While Noel's parents were rich, Noel mostly got away with getting free stuff because of his association.

"I'm so glad you suggested this cruise," Anna said. "It's already been so much fun. The ship is great too. I was expecting to feel like a sardine, but I don't."

Meesha chuckled. "I know, right?"

Tim tilted his head. "You picked the cruise?"

"Uh, no, more like I picked the ship and then suggested the cruise destination. It was one of the largest ships and I thought it'd be good for not only couples but those with families too since it featured themed rooms and plenty of activities for the small kids."

Tim held her gaze. "How thoughtful." His tone almost seemed clipped, but she quickly dismissed it as bias. It wasn't his fault he reminded her of her ex.

Anna wrinkled her eyebrows as she looked at Tim and then slightly shook her head, returning her attention to Meesha. "So, what are you guys doing after this?"

Shrugging, Meesha looked at Sawyer. "I don't know. Maybe just taking a walk along the beach?" It'd be fun and it'd give him a reason to take his shoes off.

His smile reached his eyes. "I'd enjoy that. It's been a while since I've been to the beach."

Oh, those lips were so kissable, and now that she knew how soft they were, it only made them more so. "We can take our shoes off, dig our toes into the sand."

He touched his lips to her forehead. "Sounds like a plan."

How could such a small gesture give her butterflies? He was only pretending, but it seemed her body had no idea how to distinguish between real and fake. "Good.

"Is it a romantic stroll or would you mind company?" Anna asked. "I've been wanting to catch up with you. I know I was being a pain during the committee meetings, but…" She sighed. "I was stressed and not handling things well. I've apologized to the other members, but I felt like I owed you more."

Say what? Had she been body snatched? Instead of blurting that out, Meesha smiled and politely said, "It's okay."

"No, it really isn't. I'm so used to being the one giving out assignments to my junior designers and doing things my way that I was inconsiderate of everyone, including you. That's why I was so excited to add a few things to the list. I knew how hard you worked on the cruise and all the planning. I didn't contribute nearly as much as I should have. It was my way of apologizing."

Under the table, Meesha pinched herself. Never in a

million years would she have expected an apology from Anna. "I don't know what to say."

Anna touched her arm. "I just hope you can forgive me. You were always the sweetest person in high school." She looked at Sawyer. "I doubt Meesha even remembers this, but when I transferred to her school near the end of eighth grade, some of the girls were picking on me, and out of nowhere, Meesha appeared. She pushed through them, gave them what for, and that was the last day they messed with me."

Utterly floored. "I sort of remember that." She tilted her head. "That was you?"

Sawyer chuckled. "That doesn't surprise me."

Rolling his eyes, Tim sighed. "It's a little too mushy for me."

Anna waved him off and grinned. "That's why I joined all the clubs and after school stuff. You were my hero and I just wanted to be like you."

"But you beat me at everything."

"I didn't know it at the time, but I have a social anxiety disorder that was finally diagnosed when I was in college. It makes it hard for me to read social cues and engage with people my age. I've worked with a therapist for a while, but when I'm stressed, like I was during our meetings, it worsens and I kind of spiral. I'm so sorry."

Meesha's jaw dropped. "I thought you hated me."

"Not at all. I wanted to impress you, but sometimes I don't think that's how it came across." Anna lowered her gaze. "I'm so sorry I made you feel that way."

"Oh, Anna. If anyone owes an apology, it's me. All this time, I thought…"

What did she say? How could she apologize for all the horrible things she'd thought and said about Anna this whole time? "Well, I thought wrong. I'm so sorry for my part in all this. For all the negative things I've thought or said or any of the times I behaved like a spoiled brat. I hope you can forgive me."

She smiled. "Absolutely," she said, tears welling in her eyes. "I should have said something during the meetings, but…it feels weird and sometimes when I tell people about my anxiety, they dismiss it or feel sorry for me. I hate that."

Chuckling, Meesha nodded, understanding it more than she could convey. "Oh, I know how that feels."

Anna laughed. "Can we be friends? I'll do my best to keep my anxiety in check."

Smiling, Meesha nodded. "I would love to have you as my friend."

Almost like they were reading each other's mind, they stood and hugged each other. Meesha wished she could go back and change so many things. There was also part of her that wanted to come clean about her relationship with Sawyer, but not without talking to him first.

During their meal, they caught up on their lives and it was more fun than Meesha thought possible. Even Sawyer and Tim joined in, although Tim seemed to have an edge to his voice most of the time. Anna explained it was part of his humor, but that edge seemed to point in Meesha and Sawyer's direction often. She'd misjudged Anna for years, though, and she didn't want to be guilty of that again.

After their meal, they continued their conversation as they walked the beach, shoes dangling in their hands. It'd been subtle, but Meesha saw the relief in his eyes and features as he'd taken his shoes off.

The clear water, the balmy breeze, and the relaxed atmosphere worked together to make the place magical. Plus, she'd had a reason to hold his hand. He was there to keep her safe, and she felt that way even when he was just close by, but holding his hand gave that assurance an anchor.

As they were passing a large cluster of trees not too far from the shore, Anna stopped and clasped her hands together. "Wouldn't this be a perfect spot for a selfie? It's beautiful and with the shading, we won't have to deal with red eyes."

Meesha looked at Sawyer. "Sure."

He nodded. "It's good by me."

Tim stuffed his hands in his pockets. "The quicker we get this list done the better."

"He hates having his picture taken." Anna sighed. "Do you mind if we go first?"

Shaking her head, Meesha said, "Not at all."

Anna and Tim cuddled together, posing in different ways including a goofy one where Anna dipped Tim. It gave them all a good laugh.

Meesha looked over her phone. "One more, okay?"

Tim took Anna by the hand, twirled her around, and dipped her before kissing her. Cupping her cheek, he kissed her, and said, "Mon, amor."

The color drained from Meesha's face. Those two words soured her stomach. She blinked a few times and shook her head, trying to clear it. Mon amor wasn't exclusively Noel's. Anna was a fashion designer. France was the birthplace of the fashion industry, and she'd said they'd gone to France only a few months ago to do a show.

Sawyer leaned in. "Everything okay?"

She waved him off. "Oh yeah. It's pretty warm and I probably haven't had enough water."

His eyes narrowed as his gaze roamed over her face. "When we get back to the ship, you can tell me just how much water you need." Between the lines, that translated into he wasn't buying what she was selling.

"Okay." She refocused on Tim and Anna. "I'm sorry, I didn't get the shot. Could you do it again?"

Tim groaned, but instead of voicing his frustration, he twirled Anna again, this time leaving off the mon amor.

Anna practically skipped across the small distance and stood next to Meesha, looking at the photos. "These look great."

She nodded. "You guys make a super cute couple."

"Okay, your turn!" Anna pulled her phone from her pocket.

Sawyer and Meesha took their spot. "Your face is still pale," he said, wrapping his arm around her waist and pulling her flush against him.

Palming his chest, she leaned into him. "Noel would use mon amor a lot. Hearing that just brought back bad memories. That's all. I'm okay." She smiled. "Actually, I needed to thank you for pushing me to be a better person. I'm not sure I would have joined them if it wasn't for you."

"No way I believe that. You're kind from the top of your head to the tip of your toes. All I did was nudge a little."

Her cheeks warmed. Lifting a fraction, she pressed her lips to his cheek. "You've made so many sacrifices for me. Going on this trip as my…plus one, wearing shoes that I know you hate, and you've done all of it with a smile on your face. I'm not sure how you measure yourself, but in my book, you pass with flying colors."

Crashing waves, the birds, and every other distraction faded as he caught her gaze. "I'm not so sure about that. If you knew…" So much anguish coated the words.

"I know you have a good heart. That is a fact."

He pushed her hair over her shoulder, set his hand on her shoulder, and slid it down her arm. "This hasn't been a sacrifice," he said, his voice dropping low as he leaned in closer.

Be still her heart. His lips were right there. A little lift was all it would take, and she'd be kissing him. Oh, she so wanted to kiss him. More than she'd ever wanted to kiss anyone in her life.

A phone ringing broke the moment, and she felt sideswiped. Tim yanked his phone out of his pocket and checked the screen. "Sorry, I have to take this."

"Okay." Anna smiled and he gave him a quick kiss. "He's a senior partner with a law firm. I'm in talks with them to create a cosmetic line with a large company. He's been handling it and he's always getting calls." She glanced at him as he walked away. "He's been so wonderful to me."

"I'm glad you found someone who cares about

you." Even if she was struggling with liking him. If he was good to Anna, that was all that mattered.

"All right, scooch together. I got a couple already, but one more for good measure, right?"

Meesha hugged Sawyer around the waist. "Right."

"Talk about a cute couple." Anna crossed the distance and held up her phone. "It was like you were in your own world."

"How about we get a photo of the two of us?" asked Meesha.

"Sure." Meesha looked at Sawyer.

He held up his hand. "Say no more. I've got you." He chuckled and they gave him their phones.

Anna and Meesha struck a pose and just as Sawyer went to lift the camera, two men emerged from the left, slamming into him and throwing him onto the ground. After that, everything was a blur of fists and feet and screams.

The man who'd taken Sawyer to the ground, wrestled with him while his partner approached Meesha and Anna. Meesha quickly dug into the front pocket of her bag and pulled out her safety keychain, brandishing her pepper spray. "Come any closer and I will empty this cannister."

As if she was bluffing, the man continued to advance and she smashed the lever, blasting the man in the face. He yelled and ducked. Apparently, giving

Sawyer the distraction he needed. He delivered a quick roundhouse kick, dropping the man to the ground where he laid still. Before the man coming for Meesha or Anna could reach them, Sawyer grabbed him by the arm and swung him around.

They exchanged several blows before Sawyer's fist landed a solid shot across the man's jaw. He dropped to the ground, quickly scrambled to his feet, and ran as soon as he realized his buddy was completely out.

"Help!" Anna screamed, seeming to find her voice. "Help!"

Tim slid to a stop; his eyes wide as he seemed to process the scene. He began yelling for help in unison with Anna. Finally, what looked like a local bounded over, realized what had happened, and called for the police.

Sawyer raced to Meesha and took her face in his hands. "Are you okay? You aren't hurt anywhere, are you?" His eyebrows knitted together. "I'm so sorry. I didn't even see them coming." He pulled her into a bear hug, holding her like she was the most precious thing on the earth.

"I'm fine," she replied, wrapping her arms around him. He could have been seriously hurt, and it was all because of her. Leaning back, her heart sank as she looked him over. He was already sporting the beginnings of one black eye, an ugly gash near his hairline, a cut on his bottom lip, and his shirt was torn. "We need to get you checked out."

His lips lifted on one corner. "I'm just fine as long as you're okay."

Well, physically maybe, but emotionally, not so much. She'd known him all of a couple of days, and she'd liked him from the second she met him. He'd saved her life, putting himself firmly in the hero category. The arrow on her like meter ticked upward. If this kept up, her heart was going to be in serious jeopardy.

10

"I promise I'm fine." Sawyer's feet dangled as he sat on the edge of a gurney as one of the medics, Badrick, examined him. "Really. There's no reason to fuss." He touched the bandage covering the cut on his forehead and grimaced. When the guy slammed into him, he'd hit a piece of driftwood sticking out of the sand and given himself a nasty cut.

One minute he'd been taking a picture of Meesha and Anna, the next, he was eating sand. It'd come out of nowhere. Not once had he ever found himself *that* caught off guard and it could have cost Meesha her life too. He'd let Tru, Kayleigh, and Meesha down.

Instead of being aware of his surroundings, he'd been too preoccupied with thoughts he shouldn't be having. If Tim's phone hadn't rung... things could have turned out much different.

"There is a reason to fuss. If you hadn't stopped that man, there's no telling what he would've done."

A local shop owner had heard the screaming, and he'd called the police to report the mugging. Well, for now, that's what the police were calling it. He didn't have anything solid to suggest otherwise either. Airing on the side of caution, he'd called Ryder, given him the location, and a brief rundown of events. Perhaps there were security cameras that Ryder could use to get more information. At the moment, there was nothing that could point to the attack as being anything other than a random attempted mugging. That didn't assuage his guilt at all.

The medic on scene finished bandaging the cut on his cheek. "I'm going to let the police know they can get your statement. I'll return to check on you when I'm finished."

"Thank you," Meesha said.

In the distance, Tim had his arms around Anna as they gave the police their statements. It'd taken more than a few soothing words to calm her down. Unlike Meesha who seemed to be completely unfazed.

The guy who'd slammed into him got him right in the kidney, and he suspected a bruise was already forming. "It's not as bad as it looks, and I've dealt with worse." He shifted on the gurney and his gaze lowered to the ground. "You could've been hurt. I wasn't—"

"Stop." She stepped closer to him. "If anyone has a reason to feel guilty about something, it's me. I'm the reason you're here. If I hadn't been so petty, we wouldn't be here, and you wouldn't be hurt."

"You don't know that. If Noel has access to the funds you think he has, he could have very well sent someone to Myrtle Beach. At least these two guys weren't professionals." He looked down at himself. "Honestly, it could have been much worse."

"What?" The question came out breathless.

Apparently, he'd said the wrong thing because when he looked up, she looked stricken. "I just mean, this is what I do. It's part of the job and this isn't the first time I've been in a fight."

She cupped his face. "That doesn't mean I have to like it. Doesn't mean I don't want to take care of you or sooth your wounds. Selfless people like you need even more care because you empty yourself for other people and sometimes you need help refilling."

His lungs felt squeezed. No one had ever said anything like that to him before. Oh, his clients had thanked him, but this was a new level. "Uh…"

Like a feather, Meesha touched her lips to the cut on his lip and repeated the soft, agonizing ghost-like kisses until she'd kissed every cut on his face. "I'm going to take care of you, and you're going to let me. Got it?"

Suddenly, he wished he'd let that guy work his face over a little more. He swallowed hard. "Got it." He choked out.

"Good," she said, and her lips quirked into the most stunning smile he'd seen to date. It went to her eyes, filled her face with warmth, and he could swear a halo was hovering above her head.

"Are you always this dedicated to taking care of people?"

"Only people I like, and I definitely like you." She winked.

In his head, he was on his knees, offering his heart up on a silver platter. If this was like, love had to be something he couldn't conceive. "I like being liked." He lowered his head as the words echoed in the air between his ears. *Like to be liked?* He was a twenty-nine-year-old man acting like a high school moron. "I mean, thank you."

Her lips rolled in, like she was fighting a smile. "I know what you meant."

Before he could respond, Anna and Tim stopped next to them. Anna covered Sawyer's hand with hers. "Thank you for rescuing us. I thought that man was for sure going to hurt us."

Tim nodded. "I owe you a deep thanks." He squeezed Anna to him. "If something happened to her, I'd be lost."

Sawyer sort of expected that from Anna, but Tim? That was a surprise. So far, he hadn't shown much affection, at least not publicly. Not that he wouldn't appreciate Sawyer keeping his girlfriend safe, but that he'd voice it.

"It really wasn't that big of a deal."

"Oh, yes, it was. It was a huge deal." Anna sniffed. "I was so stunned at first, I was frozen."

Tim looked at Sawyer. "Where did you learn to fight like that?"

Working for a security firm, he'd found it wise to downplay his skill. Shrugging, he said, "Uh, I was in karate until I went to high school. I guess it's like riding a bicycle."

Tim nodded. "Guess so. Good thing for us you remembered too."

Just then, a man in uniform joined them. "We've taken the man who attacked you into custody, and we'll be interrogating him soon." He nodded his head in the direction of the cruise ship. "If it's okay with you, I'd like to get your statements now."

Meesha's description of the altercation was much like Sawyer's without the fists. While he'd been fighting with the man who slammed into him, Meesha had used pepper spray, but the man advancing on them seemingly dodged it. That's when Sawyer knocked his assailant out and grabbed the guy trying to get to Meesha and Anna. They'd traded a few blows, and he'd eventually run off.

The officer continued scribbling a few more notes and looked up. "Any distinguishing marks on the one who ran away?"

Meesha and Sawyer shook their heads. "No, not that I could see, but everything happened so fast," Meesha said.

"I got a glimpse of what looked like a tattoo on his chest, but I can't tell you what it was."

"Okay." The man put his notebook in his pocket. "Well, we have everyone's statements, so you're free to go now. If we find out anything, we'll let you know."

Sawyer shook his hand. "Thank you." He slipped off the gurney and stood.

The medic looked from Sawyer to Meesha. "If anything changes, if you feel dizzy or nauseous, you'll need to see a doctor. Okay?"

"I'll keep an eye on him, and if anything changes," Meesha said, eyeing Sawyer, "I'll take him to the ships infirmary."

With the way she was looking at him, there was no doubt in his mind that her students kept themselves in line. "And I'll go peacefully." Maybe if he was tranquilized.

Meesha caught his gaze and narrowed her eyes as if

she could sense what was going through his mind. A second later, a lone eyebrow ticked upward. "We'll discuss the definition of peacefully when we get to the cabin."

Yeah, he'd known falling for her wouldn't take any effort, and he'd been right. He grinned. "Yes, ma'am."

It'd been years since he'd allowed himself even a second to revisit what happened during that ambush in Afghanistan. He'd killed a civilian, a man he'd called a friend. Everything had happened so quickly and in moments they were exchanging fire with rebels. Maybe…

He shoved the thought away. Meesha was a once in a lifetime woman, and she needed a once in a lifetime kind of man. Even if she gave him a pass on murder, he still had a job that took him all over the world and put him in dangerous situations. Would it be fair to ask that of her? That was assuming she was interested in him.

She seemed to be, but it was a cruise, and they were pretending. Not exactly the best start for anything remotely serious, and for him, it'd be serious. He'd been all or nothing since he was a kid.

Honestly, he wasn't sure why he was giving it any thought at all. He needed to concentrate on keeping her safe not keeping her in his arms. Once this cruise was over, things would go back to normal. She'd return to Myrtle Beach, he'd hide in his room at Guardian Group, and all would end well.

11

Meesha leaned against the balcony railing while Sawyer rested in his room. As she scanned the area that stretched in front of her, she was in awe of the number of stars. It was like someone had taken a bucket of glitter and tossed it. While she loved living in the city, she couldn't deny the beauty or the peacefulness of an endless, twinkling night sky.

Closing her eyes, the events of the day played in color. Everything had happened so quickly. One minute they were taking photos for the scavenger hunt, and the next, Sawyer was being thrown to the ground and a large man was storming towards her.

She'd gone from carefree to frozen in a blink, but all those self-defense classes had paid off, or so she thought. The pepper spray didn't even faze the man. He'd just bulldozed right on through like a Terminator. If it weren't for Sawyer swooping in to rescue her, it chilled her to the bone to wonder what might have happened. He'd fought both men, and his poor face took the brunt of the tussle. His bottom lip was cut. He had a black eye and a gnarly gash near his hairline.

The look on his face after she'd kissed each of his wounds tickled her. Not that she'd planned it, but she'd reasoned that it's what a girlfriend would do. Then his eyes, wide as saucers, and the way he responded with *I like to be liked* was too cute.

Once he was checked out and they'd given their statements, it was a mad dash to make it back to the ship on time. Before parting ways, they'd made plans to meet Anna and Tim for breakfast the next day, if Sawyer felt up to it. Of course, he'd played it down like it was nothing.

Not unexpected since he'd brushed off his injuries from the very beginning. She'd been horrified when he said they were part of the job. Of course, logically she understood that because what he did was dangerous, but that didn't make her heart hurt any less.

That pull she felt when she first met him was growing stronger by the minute. Some of it she could attribute to being rescued by him, but not all of it. If it weren't for him nudging her to be a better person, she'd still be stuck in a one-sided contest with Anna. She certainly wouldn't have made friends with her. Beyond the physical attraction, which would be a lie to ignore, she liked the way she felt when she was with him. She couldn't remember a time when she felt so safe with a man. After Noel, what she wanted more than anything was to feel secure both emotionally and physically. Good looks and great smiles only went so far. She wanted substance and depth…and Sawyer seemed to be perfect. Well, not perfect. No one was perfect. He sure was close though.

Taking a deep breath in, the warm, salty air filled her lungs and she shut the thoughts down. All these thoughts needed to stop. She was still shaken up by what happened, and it wasn't the right time to think about relationships or anything related to it.

Just as she closed her eyes, intending to take another deep breath, the bark of a *no* caught her ear. She hurried inside the cabin, stopping at Sawyer's door right as he let out another *no* followed by a whimper.

She crossed the room and turned on the side table lamp as she sat beside him. Based on the pained expression, his damp hair, and the way the sheets were twisted, it was obvious he was having a nightmare. She touched his arm. "Sawyer?"

He bolted upright, dragging his hand through his sweat soaked hair as he panted. His eyebrows knitted together. "I'm sorry."

"It's okay."

"No, I should have warned you." He took a couple of big breaths and let them out slowly. When he spoke again, his voice was a little steadier. "It's been long enough since I had one that I thought I was in the clear. Apparently, I was wrong."

Tilting her head, her eyebrows knitted together. "How long has it been?"

Sawyer shrugged. "I don't know. Maybe six months. I guess today…" The sentence trailed off as he caught her gaze again.

"Today triggered it." Now she felt like an even bigger heel. First, he got hurt and now he'd had a nightmare. The selfish part of her wanted to ask him about it, but he was giving her that same anguished look from earlier. If he decided to share it, it'd be voluntary. Not because she asked. "Is there anything I can do for you?"

His stomach growled. "Something to eat?" He smacked his lips. "A drink too?"

"Absolutely."

As she stood, he swung his legs over the side of the bed and pushed off. "I'll be out in a minute."

"Okay. I'll call room service. Anything sound good?"

He shrugged. "Something simple. Burger and fries."

"You got it." She walked out of the room and straight to the phone sitting on the desk. It wasn't until she started ordering that she realized her lunch was long gone.

As she curled up on the end of the loveseat, Sawyer walked out of his room, towel drying his hair. How did he manage to look like he was walking off a modeling shoot every time she saw him? Even in just a t-shirt and pajama pants he gave her butterflies.

Yawning, he took a seat at the opposite end. "How are you feeling?"

Her? She wasn't the one who'd been beaten up. "I don't know. A little shaken still?" She framed it as a question more than a statement. "Overall, okay. How are you feeling?"

"A little sore, but only because it's been a while since I was in a close combat situation." He draped the towel over the arm of the chair, grumbling to himself so low she only caught the end of what he was saying. "I should've—"

"Done what? It's not like any of us weren't surprised by the attack. I didn't see anyone around, and I was paying attention. When I took my self-defense class, one of the biggest things emphasized was being aware of your surroundings." She set her elbow against the couch and put her head in her hand. "We even did live training for it."

"Tru?"

Nodding, she said, "And Kayleigh, but I was already researching classes. I wanted to make sure I was taught more than a couple of moves."

Facing her, he nodded. "That was smart. It's easy to practice that type of stuff, but if you don't know how to apply it to real world situations, it doesn't mean much."

"Exactly. Even with all that experience, I still froze for a second. Although, with the way the guy just waltzed through the pepper spray, I think I might need to upgrade to something stronger. I have a taser but those aren't allowed on a cruise."

He laughed. "Yeah, I keep grabbing for my service weapon, and it's not there. Makes it a little more interesting to keep you safe."

"When did you learn jujitsu?" She'd only caught a little of his fight, but that kick he used to knock out the one guy was pretty impressive.

"After basic training. One of my buddies had trained since he was a kid, had a ton of awards from competitions, and offered to teach me if I wanted to learn. I took him up on it, and I was hooked by the end of the first lesson."

She nodded. "The class I took didn't focus on just one type of defense. My instructor thought it was best if we knew a variety that way if an attacker knew how to block one type, we could switch things up and catch them off guard."

A smile quirked on his lips. "That sounds like an incredible class."

"It was, and I recommend it to everyone. It did more than teach me self-defense, it taught me the confidence to use the self-defense." She lifted her head and dropped her hand to her lap. "How long did it take you to get your black belt?"

"About four years. I was a wrestler, and so it took me less time than most."

"Do you still keep in contact with your friend?"

He gave a slight shake of his head. "No, uh, once I left the Army, I kind of let all of my relationships go."

Catching his gaze, she closed the small distance. Again, there was such a depth of anguish it nearly drowned her. He'd rescued her twice in the span of days, and oh, what she'd give to rescue him. "I take it there's a story there?"

"There is, but I don't like to talk about it." The reply was so soft, if she wasn't mere inches from him, she wouldn't have heard it. "You may not want me protecting you if you knew."

It wasn't just what he said that broke her heart, it was the way he said it and the hopelessness that coated the words. She understood that more than he could possibly know. When she'd returned from Paris, she'd been a shell. Honestly, she still felt that way at times.

Circling her arms around his neck, she whispered, "That's not true. I will never believe that."

For a moment, he stiffened and then gave a long, soft sigh, wrapping his arms around her, holding onto her as tightly as she was holding onto him. The way he held her felt so different than the way Noel had held her, it was a completely different experience. With Sawyer, it felt like he wanted and needed her. It didn't feel selfish or possessive.

The longer they held each other, the thicker the air grew. Finally, she leaned back, and the world fell away. As their eyes met, his held such an intensity, her pulse jumped. He took his arm from around her, palmed the side of her face, and his thumb brushed across her lips.

Just as she thought he'd kiss her; a knock came from the door. He blinked like he'd been under a spell and untangled himself. "Uh…we should get that."

"Yeah, we should," she said, nodding.

The second his back was to her; she palmed the spot over her heart. She wasn't sure if the interruption thrilled her or broke her heart. A few soft breaths, and she decided it was probably for the best.

She liked Sawyer, but being forced into close quarters made for a murky emotional field of landmines. It was better for them to get through this cruise and end it as friends. Expecting anything more than that was a good way to get her heart broken, and she'd experienced enough of that to last her a lifetime.

12

He'd almost kissed her. The near-disaster scenario played in Sawyer's head once more, and if he wasn't sitting in a cable car on the way to the top of Mount Isabel de Torres, Puerto Plata, with her, Anna and Tim, he'd be kicking himself for even getting himself into the situation to begin with.

At first, he'd wanted to punch whoever knocked on the door, but once his head was clear, he was half-tempted to find the concierge and give her a high five. She'd saved his keister big time. If he kissed Meesha, there was no doubt in his mind that he'd never want to stop.

They'd eaten together in awkward silence, and then she'd disappeared into her room. When she'd walked out of her room the next morning, he'd wondered if she'd had as hard a time falling asleep as he did since she was sporting circles as dark as his around her eyes.

He'd half expected the awkwardness to continue, but she'd marched right over to him, looked him in the eyes, and clucked like a mother hen over the bruises on his face. Once he'd assured her he was okay and fit for sightseeing, they'd met up with Anna and Tim for a quick breakfast before disembarking from the ship.

"Whew. It's warm. Glad we're doing this first thing rather than waiting until later." Smiling, Meesha lifted a little and looked out the cable car window.

Anna chuckled. "No kidding."

Sweat beaded Tim's hairline and he ran his hand over his forehead. "I'm not a hot weather fan either, but the pictures make it seem like there's plenty of shade."

Anna bumped his shoulder with hers. "And plenty of romantic spots, too."

It was quick, but Meesha's lips curved down before lifting again. "Yeah, plenty." She gave a small sigh. "I loved the gardens in Paris. Well, I loved Paris."

"Paris?" Anna asked. "When were you in Paris?"

"About two years ago, I was teaching there, and...I missed my family too much, so I resigned and came home."

Tim's eyes narrowed. "Oh, did you enjoy teaching there?"

Meesha nodded. "Yeah." The word came out just above a whisper.

Sawyer put his arm around her, pulling her closer, hoping to, in some small way, give her support and comfort. "She's an incredible teacher, and the kids loved her."

She lifted her gaze to his, a bright blanket of pink on her cheeks. "He's just being sweet."

"No, I'm not. You're *fantastic*. Patient, kind, and caring, and the kids know it."

Anna grinned. "I don't doubt that at all. Meesha was the sweetest person when we were in school. Everyone loved her."

Waving her off, Meesha shook her head. "I don't remember it that way."

"Well, of course, you don't. You weren't snobbish or stuck up. You were just…you." She turned to Tim. "Her oldest sister, Kayleigh suffered a horrible fall off their roof during Christmas one year, and Meesha advocated for special needs students during our entire four years in high school. So much so, that our school received a reward for being the most special needs friendly in the area."

Pride swelled in Sawyer's chest. "That's my girl." Something he was wishing for more and more the longer he was around her. A wish that needed to be buried six feet under because it couldn't happen.

"Did you teach special needs in Paris?" asked Anna.

"I wouldn't call them special needs. More like walking to the beat of their own drum. They had sensitivities that required a little more patience and creativity when it came to educating."

Anna nodded. "So not surprised at all."

Meesha's cheeks took on an even deeper blush. With that, they sat in companionable silence until they reached the top of the mountain. The operator held the door as they got out.

Tim tangled his fingers in Anna's. "I don't want to seem rude, but would it be okay if Anna and I explored on our own?"

Anna bit her bottom lip, grinning like there was a surprise waiting for her.

Meesha smiled. "That's not rude." She wrapped her arms around Sawyer's chest. "I wouldn't mind a moment alone either."

Of course, she was just playing up the fake part of the relationship, and again, Sawyer had to remind himself that he couldn't entertain thoughts that took him down a road that ended with him spending the rest of his life with her. "Me either," he said, dropping a kiss on the top of her head.

"We can meet back here later, and maybe find a spot for lunch," Anna added.

"That sounds great. We'll see you guys later." Meesha waited a beat as Tim and Anna walked away, swinging their arms. She dropped her arms to her sides and sighed. "Anna said she thought he'd propose on this trip. I suspect we'll be celebrating an engagement when we meet again."

"Well, he definitely picked a romantic spot, that's for sure."

Shrugging, Meesha said, "Maybe, but I wouldn't want this. For Anna, it's perfect. I'm happy for her." She gave Sawyer a side glance. "Would you propose like this?"

Sawyer took her hand, and they began walking in the opposite direction. "Uh, well, if I ever did get engaged, I'm not sure. I've never really given it any thought." Well, before he'd killed someone he'd always seen himself taking his girl somewhere nice and then finding a quiet spot to get on one knee. Meesha had certainly dredged those thoughts up again.

"When I was a kid, I thought it was so romantic and I had this vision of what I'd want. As I've gotten older, I've realized that what I want is a simple love. After Noel, I just want a man I can trust and love who loves and trusts me. I want a no-frills, no-fuss, *will you marry me.*"

A simple kind of love. With those five words, her appeal quadrupled. Love, trust, no frills, no fuss. Talk about a love language. He shook the thought away. It made no difference. Even if there was a chance, she'd probably return to Paris to teach once Noel was out of the picture.

As if his brain had no direct connection to his mouth, he asked, "Not trying to bring up bad memories, but when Noel gets caught and you for sure know you'll never have to deal with him again, would you go back to Paris?" Like it mattered?

"When I first got back to the states, I thought about it all the time. I'd worked so hard to get the position, and I felt robbed. Honestly, I doubt the school would want me back after everything that happened."

His heart fist pumped. It had to stop. All this back and forth was giving him a headache. "You never know. It sounds like they really liked you."

"They did, but," she said, and pulled him to a stop under the shade of a tree, pointing her finger at him, "you can't say a word! Do you understand?"

He blinked. "Uh, yeah."

"You promise you will not speak a word?"

"Cross my heart." He made a motion with his finger. "And hope to die."

"Kayleigh thinks she's pregnant. She took a home test, but she wants to make sure before she tells Tru. I'm not leaving when my big sister is going to have a baby."

Dumbstruck and thrilled were the only two words running through Sawyer's mind. "That's awesome." And while he was incredibly happy for his friend, there was a part of him that shriveled with envy at the thought.

He wanted all of that. A wife, children. The swing set in the backyard, coaching t-ball, attending a ballet recital. He wanted to be a husband and a daddy. Happily living vicariously through his teammates didn't seem all that appealing anymore.

"I know, but that means I'm staying where I'm at. Honestly, I'm thinking I'm living too far away as it is, but I can't leave my kids. It's just too hard on them when a teacher quits, and I won't do that to them."

This woman. She was good all the way to her marrow. He wrapped his arms around her, squeezing her. "You are one special lady, Meesha Kingston."

She returned the hug, and he could feel her laughter tickle his heart. "And you're an extraordinary man."

"No…"

Leaning back, she took his face in her hands. "Yes. Yes, you are. You might think that volunteering to come with me is nothing, but to me, you're Superman. You did that for me, and you didn't have to. You sacrificed for me, and I can see it in your eyes every time you look at me." She smiled. "I see your heart Sawyer James, and it warms me."

His heart lodged in his throat. That was without a doubt the kindest thing anyone had ever said to him, and the fact that she was saying it meant even more to him. The modicum of remaining willpower he'd had until this point was gone. He leaned closer and touched his lips to hers, holding them there a moment before brushing his lips across hers.

She shuddered, melting against him as her arms circled his neck. Again and again, he brushed his lips across hers before nipping at her bottom lip and deepening the kiss. The soft moan followed by her hands threading through his hair kindled a fire in his belly.

When his lungs became desperate for air, he broke the kiss unaware of how long they'd stood there. It wasn't until their eyes met that he realized he'd just complicated things. He'd kissed her without telling her about his past. Who he was, what he'd done, and the guilt hit him full force.

"I shouldn't—"

"Stop," she said as she caught his gaze. "We're pretending to date. People who date, kiss. Right?"

That was true, but... Hadn't he made the argument that kissing her would lead to wanting more of her kisses? "I just... don't want to complicate things."

"You haven't. Everything's okay. We're still just...

friends." She smiled. "Just friends. We'll just pretend a little more than we initially planned. That's all."

Well, she did have a point. They were pretending to be a couple. Couples kissed. In a way, really, it was perfect. He'd get to kiss her as much as he wanted, soak her up, and at the end, he could let her go so she could find someone infinitely more worthy of her than him. It'd crush him, but if he held onto her tightly enough, kissed her enough, maybe he could burn her into his memory. "So, we just do what a normal dating couple would do, right?"

She pressed her lips to his. "Exactly. Which means, I get to hold you and kiss you and at the end of the cruise, things go back to the way they were."

He could totally handle that, his brain said with authority and assurance while his heart screamed danger. "Okay." He cupped her cheek with his hand, touched his lips to hers and immediately deepened the kiss.

Warning bells wailed and he promptly ignored them. He was going to enjoy these sweet lips, let her warmth fill all the void he'd felt the last few years, and deal with the heart-crushing consequences later. For now, he was happy, and he was going to hold onto it until he couldn't.

13

"Hey." Meesha greeted Anna as she came into view. A few feet away Tim had his phone in his ear with his lips turned down and one hand on his hip. It was a pretty good indication that he wasn't happy with whoever happened to be on the other line.

After spending a couple of hours enjoying the beach, Meesha and Sawyer had returned to the preplanned meeting spot. Although, now that their fake dating came with very real kisses, she was almost sad she'd suggested it.

Oh, his kisses.

Inwardly, she sighed and did a twirl *Sound of Music* style. There weren't words to give that kiss justice. She was still floating on cloud nine and her bruised lips only wanted more. It went beyond just a kiss too. The way he'd looked at her. The way he'd held her. How was any future kiss supposed to compete with that humdinger of a fantasy come true? The very thought of kissing another man made her nose turn up.

She'd seen the look of retreat in his eyes as well, and the first thing to come to her mind was that they were pretending. The spur of the moment, desperate thought had flashed in her mind, and she'd gone with it. She'd play along, pretending all of it was fake, but there was no way he'd ever convince her that he was faking it. She certainly wasn't faking the way she returned his kisses.

More than once he'd commented that she wouldn't want a man with his past. Even if he had committed some horrible wrong, what were the statutes of limitations? Did it mean he was doomed to live alone for the rest of his life? Where does mercy or grace factor in there?

She stuffed her hand in her pocket, touched the ring Noel had given her and wrapped her hand around it. It was the last piece of Noel she had. Before leaving Paris, she'd thrown everything away, and she couldn't for the life of her figure out why she hadn't immediately tossed it overboard that first night.

Her gaze dipped to Anna's ring finger, finding it just as barren now as it was at the beginning of the day.

Meesha tipped her head in Tim's direction. "Is everything okay?"

Anna nodded. "Yeah, he's got a huge investment deal in the works, and his client is a little needy."

Tim turned just then, did a wave, and returned his focus to the phone call, tapping his fingers against his lips. For a moment, Meesha was frozen in place. One of Noel's nervous habits was tapping his fingers against his lips. She shook her head. Noel looked nothing like Tim, and he was at least three inches taller. It wasn't like people didn't share ticks, and finger tapping was common.

"Oh, okay." She smiled. Perhaps that client had been interrupting too much for Tim to pop the question. Obviously, she wasn't going to bring it up just in case she'd read things wrong. "I overheard a couple talking about a restaurant right on the beach with rave reviews. Does that sound good to you?"

Anna gasped. "That'd be great, especially after what happened yesterday." She looked at Sawyer. "Are you still feeling okay?"

"Yeah, I'm fine."

Meesha's gaze roamed his face. "A little sore and tired." She'd noticed that his gait was off and the little grimaces he'd given here and there as they walked through the garden.

"What?" he asked as he tilted his head.

"Just little things I've noticed today." She stepped closer and combed her fingers through his hair. "I mean, I'm supposed to be keeping a close eye on you, right?"

He took her hand and kissed her palm. "Thank you." Leaning in, he set his mouth to her ear. "For seeing me."

Holy smokes, what this man did to her. "Always."

Tim returned, hooking his arm around Anna's waist. "Sorry. Clients don't tend to understand vacations sometimes."

Sawyer waved him off. "Eh, no apologies needed."

Meesha shivered as Tim's gaze hit hers. When would this icky feeling about him go away? He'd done nothing to her, and the fact that he reminded her of Noel wasn't his fault. "We were just talking about lunch. Apparently, there's a beachside restaurant with great food."

Tim nodded. "Sounds good to me."

After an hour's wait for the cable car, they returned to the base of the mountain and took a taxi to the restaurant. To say it was beautiful was…well, Meesha couldn't find a word to accurately describe it. Soft sand, inviting water, and a cool breeze made for an ideal location for a meal.

"Oh, this is nice," Anna said, sitting back in her chair. "And the food smells fantastic."

"Honestly, I think I could eat shoe leather." Meesha laughed.

Sawyer nodded. "Yeah, breakfast hit the road hours ago."

A waiter stopped at their table, took their drink orders, and dropped off menus.

In unison, they opened them, and their conversation grew lively as they discussed the different entrees. National dishes such as La Bandera, which was red beans, rice, stewed meats and fried green plantains, to fish with coconut sauce called samaná's pescado con coco, along with freshly fried pork rinds were offered.

"Oh, there's too many choices," Anna said and sighed. "I want to try everything." She laughed.

Meesha chuckled. "Yeah, me too."

"We could each get a different dish, and share." Sawyer shrugged.

Tim closed his menu and set it down. "I'm okay with that."

Anna nodded. "Sounds good to me."

By the time the waitress returned, they'd made their choices and gave her their orders. When she was out of earshot, Tim leaned back and laid his arm across the back of Anna's chair.

"Meesha, you said you taught in Paris. Did you teach primary, junior secondary, or college?" Tim asked with a slight French accent on the last word. It was so minor that if someone hadn't lived in Paris, they may not have even caught it.

"Do you speak French?" Meesha asked.

He shook his head. "No." He paused and added. "I took French in high school, but it wasn't my favorite subject." He held her gaze. "Did you pick up the language while you lived there?"

She shrugged. "Yes, actually, fairly quickly. I'd taken it in high school and when I applied to the school, I began studying right away in case I was offered the position."

The staring match held to a point of discomfort until Meesha pulled away and looked at Anna. "How did you guys meet?"

Anna smiled up at him, chuckling. "I was looking to move, and when I arrived at the showing with my realtor, Tim was there. He'd gotten his times mixed up. We hit it off, and the rest is history."

"Best day of my life." Tim took her chin in his fingers, touched his lips to Anna's, and brushed the tip of his nose across hers. "Mon amor, my Anna."

Mon amor, my Anna? The way he said it... Meesha squirmed in her seat.

Anna bit her bottom lip. "One of the sexiest things he picked up in France."

"France?" The word came out a little breathy.

"I had a show in Milan, and he surprised me by

flying to France and taking me out for our one-month anniversary. A total surprise. It was the sweetest, most romantic thing anyone had ever done. No one had ever done that before, and I hadn't even given it any thought." She leaned into him. "But he did. I was head over heels from that point forward."

With a shrug, Tim gazed into Anna's eyes. "Because it's important to celebrate even the small things when you care about someone."

An involuntary shiver ran down Meesha's spine. Once upon a time, she would have considered that sweet and romantic, but it was like hearing Noel using Tim's voice. If she was sure she wouldn't have to explain gagging, that's exactly what she'd be doing. Why did the guy have to remind her so much of Noel?

After a moment, Anna broke eye contact with Tim and looked at Meesha. "How about you and Sawyer?"

"Her sister works for the same company I do," Sawyer replied, smiling as he looked at Meesha. "She burst through the door one day and that was it for me. I knew the second her eyes locked with mine, life as I know it would change."

Boy, the way he said it, she'd put her five bucks down for whatever he might be selling. "I was so involved in the conversation I was having with my sister that I didn't even see him at first." She gave a soft laugh, sighed, and their eyes met. It wasn't a lie to say she felt peace when she was around him. He made her heart beat faster, her skin clammy, and butterflies would go wild in her stomach. She tilted her head and palmed his cheek. "I turned around and the world just…just fell away. He was the most attractive man I'd ever seen. If you'd asked me if I believed in love at first sight, I'd have laughed, and now, he's challenged that since the day I met him. He has the most incredibly kind heart."

Sawyer's Adam's apple bobbed as he swallowed. The torrent of emotions reflecting in his eyes made her wish they were at dinner alone. A moment later, he pressed his face into her hand. "My luckiest day ever was meeting you."

Obviously, he was just playing it up, but it sure didn't feel that way.

"How sweet." Tim said, the last word coming out sharp, almost sounding like it was dripping with disdain.

Sawyer blinked like he'd been in a trance and smiled. "Yeah, she is."

Meesha looked at Tim, noting his relaxed face in direct opposition to the contempt in his voice. In fact, he seemed happy, almost elated with a wide smile on his face. Man, she had to stop comparing him to Noel as if her ex was the only guy to ever be romantic.

Frustration built in her chest as she fought down

anger. The only way she was ever going to move on was to excise her ex, totally and completely. Maybe she'd start with that ring. She'd mentally attach all the baggage to it, toss it overboard, and maybe her path to a new groove would grow exponentially easier.

Perhaps this time it'd stick, and she could once and for all, be done with Noel and move on with her life.

14

Meesha's reunion group had left the ship together to explore Coral World Ocean Park. Along with dolphins, there were sea turtles, diving, an aviary, and plenty of exhibits to visit. They'd been split into groups of ten with Sawyer, Meesha, Anna and Tim in the second group.

"I have to say, this swimming with dolphins thing is pretty cool." Sawyer treaded water next to Meesha as he watched some of the kids on the platform give a dolphin a belly rub.

Meesha nodded. "I know. I never thought in a million years that I'd do something like this. After being so gruff with Anna and Tim about adding it to the list of activities, I guess I owe them an apology, especially since they graciously paid for everyone."

As Sawyer watched the couple swimming in the

distance, the focus of his attention was Tim. Sawyer wasn't sure if Meesha realized it or not, but she'd been physically reacting to the guy since the cruise started. At first, he let it pass based on her history with Anna, but after two days of it, he'd called Ryder and asked him to do a double check on Tim. If Ryder found something, he'd tell Meesha. Until then, he'd keep that to himself. Ruining her cruise when it could be nothing seemed like a cruel thing to do.

"I think they know." He was mostly referring to Anna.

"Maybe, but as rude as I was, I feel like it's necessary." She glanced at him. "The kids sure seem to love it, and the staff is excellent with them. They made the rules clear and easy to understand. Even the more rambunctious children are being handled with patience."

"Yeah, everyone seems to be having a great time." He angled himself toward her. "Do you want kids? I mean, I know you teach and enjoy it, but that doesn't mean you necessarily want to be a parent." He was pretty sure he knew the answer and had a feeling she'd make a fantastic mom.

"Yeah, I do. How about you?"

"A baker's dozen." He laughed.

Her jaw dropped as her eyes widened. "That's a lot of kids."

Shaking his head, he chuckled and said, "I'm kidding. Sorta. I love kids. I've always wanted a full house."

"I bet you'll be a fantastic dad."

"Better than mine for sure." He returned his attention to the kids playing. His childhood was rife with so much neglect and abuse. There wasn't a time he could remember as a child that his parents were present. He was going to be the exact opposite. "I'm going to be at every game, dance recital, and music program." He took a deep breath. "Well, that was the plan before…" He cleared his throat. "My path changed."

She tilted her head. "Noah has children, and Kayleigh says they do just fine. Noah strikes me as the kind of man who puts family first."

More than she would ever know. Sawyer's dysfunctional family had given him a twisted idea of what family meant. His parents had chosen everything else over him, and it wasn't until he'd joined Guardian Group that he'd really had the opportunity to learn how a true, caring family worked. It'd made realizing he'd never have one that much harder to swallow.

"He does, but…"

The next second, arms circled his chest and Meesha had her cheek pressed against his skin, holding him tightly. "It's okay."

Sawyer wrapped his arms around, squeezing her.

Sweet, simple, and understanding. Man, this woman was something else. Where most women would have either pushed him to talk or given him some empty soothing words, all Meesha did was hug him and infuse him with comfort. "Thank you."

She lifted her gaze to his. "Sometimes, when I'd talk about what happened with Noel, people would want to fix it. When all I really wanted was someone to listen."

Yeah, he'd found that to be the case as well. Therapists would start out listening only to end up trying to fix things. Some things weren't fixable, and his thing definitely fell into that category. "Yeah, I've had my fair share of that, too."

"Maybe we could strike out on our own after this? We could check out one of the beaches and just take it easy." She rested her chin on his chest. "That's if you want to. We could—."

"I'd be more than okay with that." The words were out of his mouth before he'd really thought it through. Being alone with her left plenty of opportunity for kissing, and he was a lot less confident now than he was the day before.

She caught her bottom lip in her teeth as the corners lifted. "Okay." The lilt in her voice made it sound like she was the one getting the treat instead of him. "It's a date."

A date. He knew she didn't mean it as a date-date, but the word made him jittery. Eh, he needed to cool his jets. Even if it was a date, it was still just pretend. All he'd have to do was tell her about the firefight and she wouldn't even pretend anymore.

An hour later, Sawyer was thanking the guide for an experience he'd never forget. One he hadn't even known he'd had on his bucket list. Sure, he got to go amazing places when he provided protection, but he never participated in anything. At least nothing more than a nice meal in a fancy restaurant.

Anna sported a bright smile as she met Sawyer and Meesha at the entrance to the park. "That was just cool, right?"

"It was fantastic," Meesha replied. "I'm so sorry I was salty about it the other morning. I appreciate you and Tim doing this for the group."

"Water under the bridge. You were just looking out for everyone."

Tim slipped his phone into his pocket as he joined them, slipping his arm around Anna's waist. "So… have we made a plan?"

"Uh, well…" Meesha looked at Sawyer. "We want to spend some time together…alone. We could maybe meet for dinner before we return to the ship."

Anna's smile dropped for a split second, cutting her gaze to Tim. Sawyer knew what an eat dirt looked like, and if he were a betting man, Tim would have a mouthful. "Oh, that's totally okay."

"Actually, I'm glad you suggested it," Tim said. "I'm the one who keeps asking for time alone with Anna, and I was beginning to feel like you guys might think I don't want you around."

"Why? You're just going to be on the phone." Anna spat.

Tim ducked his head. "I know, and I'm sorry. I've turned my phone off." He pulled it from his pocket and showed it to her. "See? No calls. No interruptions. Just me and you. I promise."

Her posture softened. "Really?"

Sawyer caught Meesha's gaze, and he could see the awkwardness he felt. He didn't like drama to begin with, and he especially didn't like being in the middle of someone else's drama.

"Yeah, and if he gets mad, he gets mad." He pulled Anna close and pushed her hair over her shoulder. "All of my attention will be on you."

She hugged him around the waist and tiptoed to kiss him. "Good. You need a break too." She laid her head on his shoulder and looked at Meesha. "Sorry for that."

Meesha shrugged. "It's okay. I'm just glad you guys will get some time together."

"What did you guys have planned?" Tim asked.

"I think we're going to find a beach with good shade and just hang out for a while."

Tim brightened. "Oh, that sounds fun." He dropped a kiss on top of Anna's head. "This is her day, and I have some serious making up to do, so we'll be doing whatever she wants to do." He returned his gaze to Meesha. "If you're looking for a great beach, you should check out Lindquist Beach. It's a little off the beaten path and kind of private. I think you'll really like it."

Nodding, Meesha said, "Oh, well, thanks. That sounds great."

"Let me know what you think, okay?" Tim smiled. "I mean it."

She glanced at Sawyer, her eyebrows knitting together. "Uh, sure. We'll let you know."

Once they were out of earshot, Sawyer scratched the back of his neck. "That was uncomfortable."

"So, uncomfortable. I felt so weird, like I was spying."

"I don't think I'd want to air my issues like that."

Meesha shook her head. "No, never. It's not like relationships don't have problems. Nothing is ever perfect, but Anna should have talked to him in private. My parents never fought in front of us. I plan to continue the tradition."

He sure wished he'd had that privilege when he

was growing up. "Oh, yeah, my parents would have knock-down, drag-outs in front of God and everyone. I remember as a kid being at lunch with my dad's folks. Mom and Dad got into it right there in the middle of the restaurant. Got us all kicked out. I wasn't old enough to really understand what the argument was about, but definitely old enough to feel embarrassed."

She wrapped her arms around his bicep. "That sounds awful."

"Drugs and a toxic relationship." He paused. "Before they died, I finally got to see them talk to each other, even in heated battles, respectfully. In some ways, I feel like I was cheated when I lost them. I got all the bad memories and not nearly as many of the good."

"I'm sure that was…well, *is* hard."

Hard. A small word for such a big feeling. "At the time, it was and from time to time, it can hit me. Mostly, I'm thankful we got to a place that I do miss them."

"I can understand that." She squeezed his arm. "Thank you."

"For what?" he asked, truly puzzled.

"For sharing with me. You didn't have to, and you did. It's not easy talking about hard things, and we've only known each other a short time. I'm glad you felt safe enough to tell me."

Talking to her was easy. He didn't feel like he was on a couch or being scrutinized when he talked to her. There wasn't any pressure, and it didn't feel like she was digging to know whatever secret he held. It felt like she wanted to know him.

It suddenly struck him why he might have had trouble talking to therapists. At the time, he'd felt like they were only interested in picking his brain so they could fix him. When it wasn't just a head issue, it was a heart issue, and he hadn't felt like his heart was safe. Not that they'd outright said anything to make him feel that way. They were just doing what they were taught. Sometimes by the book was too scripted and he needed something a little less structured.

Or it had less to do with any of that and more to do with the growing desire to be with Meesha long after the cruise was over. He quickly quashed the idea. He didn't steal gum, he'd killed someone. It didn't matter what he wanted. What mattered was wanting what was best for her, and that best wasn't him.

15

Swimming with dolphins was one of the best things Meesha had ever experienced. Being that close to them, touching them, and learning more about them and the conservation that Coral World was doing was simply the best. She'd even had an idea for a lesson plan to include some of the things she'd learned.

Watching the kids was almost as fun as playing with dolphins. They'd been so happy. Everyone was happy, really. She couldn't imagine anyone not enjoying that experience.

Now, she was sitting in the shade with Sawyer's head in her lap, combing her fingers through his hair, and finding herself more content than she had been in a while. Instead of going straight to the beach, they'd walked around the town a little, talked, and eventually ended up at Magen's Bay instead of Lindquist.

She'd been pleasantly surprised to find the beach not nearly as packed as she'd expected. It was hands down the most beautiful beach she'd ever stepped foot on. Beautiful sand, calm, clear water, and a cute little bar and grill. The balmy breeze made it even more relaxing. "This…this is nice. I'm glad we decided to come here."

He took a deep breath and let it out slowly. "Yeah, me too." The words came out a little slurred, like he was practically on the edge of drifting off.

She cleared her throat and paused combing his hair. "I'm happy for Anna that Tim wanted to spend more time alone with her. Although, he was rather pushy about us going to Lindquist Beach." Groaning, Meesha let her head drop back. "I really should stop doing that. Thinking the worst of him. It's like I haven't patched up anything with Anna, and I'm still holding a grudge or something. Tim just…" She shivered.

Sawyer's eyes popped open, and he sat up. "Tim just…what? I've noticed a few times that he's kind of made you uncomfortable."

She waved him off but appreciated how quickly he responded. "It's nothing, really. Mostly little things that remind me of Noel. The way he looks at me sometimes, the way he talks to Anna. I mean, you've seen his picture. He doesn't even look like Noel, so I should be able to handle it."

"Have you had that happen a lot? Guys reminding you of him?" he asked, tilting his head.

"Uh, no. Not really. I think what got me was the French the other day. The way he said the words. That more than anything caught me off guard, and I think I've been hung up on that since then."

"That makes total sense. All it takes is one connection to make others stand out."

Meesha shrugged. "Yeah, maybe. I think I'm still processing this friendship with Anna." She lowered her gaze to her lap. "Since Noel, it feels like all I've been doing is trying to process things and survive."

"Well, that's understandable. What you went through with him was traumatic. As far as Anna is concerned, for more than a decade you saw her as a rival. It can take a second to recalibrate." He chuckled.

"I know, but it makes me feel guilty. She's been so sweet, and…" She paused a beat, casting her gaze to her lap. Not two hours ago, she'd given herself a pep talk. As with all of them, it was short lived. Why couldn't they stick? Why couldn't she really move on?

Blinking back tears, she said, "I feel broken. Like, something mentally and emotionally broke after everything with Noel happened. At the same time, my heart still breaks for him because I don't think he would have been the way he was if his parents had shown even an ounce of affection for him. I think he was so desperate to be loved that when he got a taste of it, he just couldn't let go."

Sawyer braced his hand in the sand as he leaned across her. "It's hard to reconcile this stuff. You had this plan for your life, and he put a wrench in it. I don't think you're broken. I think you're cautious with good reason. Once trust is lost, it's hard to recover, even if the person you want to trust is yourself."

If anything spoke to her, that did. Trusting herself was nearly impossible. But, when examining things with a critical eye, it wasn't like her instinct hadn't screamed about the red flags. Her heart had pushed her forward because she thought she could love him enough to change him, even one hundred percent knowing that wasn't the case. She just didn't like the feeling that she was giving up on someone. It'd come back to bite her, and she'd quickly learned that in the future, she needed to put her feelings down and pick up her brain. So, it wasn't necessarily trust that she had to learn, it was actually listening to herself and following through.

"It takes time to gain your confidence back too. Everything you do or say has a question mark at the end. You walk around with no conviction in your soul. You ramble and wander and wonder if you'll ever find peace." He paused a beat. "But you will. You have family and friends who love you who will help hold you up until you do. If you find yourself needing an extra pair of arms, I'm here too."

Meesha lifted her gaze to his. "Sounds like you're speaking from experience. Do you have anyone holding you up?"

"Our situations aren't the same." He lowered his gaze. "I don't deserve your compassion."

She touched her fingertips to his forehead, swept them down the side of his face, and rested them on his cheek. "Maybe you don't, but that doesn't mean I won't give it to you anyway."

"Meesha." He lifted his gaze to hers and gave a small smile. "You are the sweetest woman I've ever met. When you find the man worthy of all the things you have to offer, he'll be the luckiest man alive." The words came out like a compliment, but they felt coated in grief.

"Shouldn't I get a say in who that man might be?" she asked softly.

"Absolutely, but if that man cares about you, he wants what's best for you, even if that best isn't him. He'll put you first."

Well, Noel certainly hadn't put her first, that was for sure, and here was Sawyer, telling her that he wasn't worthy? Wouldn't that mean he was better than he was giving himself credit for? She sure thought so.

At the same time, they had just met. What if he was telling her the truth and she wasn't listening to herself like she should have with Noel? No, she didn't feel that way at all. Even if she were brutally honest, she wouldn't say she was ignoring any red flags.

"A relationship takes two people putting each other first. It's finding someone who will be a soft landing. Someone you trust when you're bruised and aching." She pushed his hair back from his face. "An ugly past doesn't automatically mean an ugly future."

He wiped his mouth with his hand, nodding. "I hear you," he said and swallowed hard.

She leaned in. "Do you?" she whispered as she touched her lips to his and held them there a moment before pulling back. Their gazes met and all she could see were storms. Keeping eye contact, she brushed her lips across his, pausing in between as their breath mingled.

In one sweeping motion, he planted his hands on each side of her face and crushed his lips to hers, immediately deepening the kiss and the intensity took her breath away. She couldn't remember ever feeling so wanted in her life.

His hands slowly left her face and found their way into her hair as the kiss continued. When he finally broke the kiss, her lungs were burning. A few gulps of air and he tilted her head back, trailing kisses from her jaw to her neck and nipping her skin with his teeth as he returned to her lips. It was an all-out assault on her nerves, and she shuddered. When had a man ever kissed her like this?

This didn't feel like a man trying to hide who he was from her. This felt like a man who was afraid of being hurt. With the way the world worked, he was justified in wanting to protect himself. Perhaps the best approach was showing Sawyer that she was someone who would protect him as much as he protected her.

He was a different kind of man. She just had to show him she was a different kind of woman.

∼

After a make out session to end all make out sessions, Meesha and Sawyer had returned to the ship to wash the day off and meet Tim and Anna for dinner right as the sun set. The call from Anna to meet them was a surprise since Tim had made such a big show of turning his phone off and promising that the entire day was hers.

"Can't say I'm not surprised Anna wanted to meet for dinner." Sawyer leaned his shoulder against the wall near the door as they waited for the couple to arrive.

She chuckled and nodded. "Yeah, I was just thinking that."

He stuffed his hands in his pockets and rolled against the wall to his back. Talk about a sexy move. He'd worn dark wash jeans and a light green shirt that brought out his eyes. She'd nearly swallowed her tongue when he walked out of his room looking like he'd walked right out of the page of a magazine.

"Maybe she's trying to make up for lost time. She knows the cruise won't last forever, and it'll be back to life as normal. Although, I don't know what normal means for a fashion designer." He shot Meesha a grin and his gaze raked down her frame. "Man, you're gorgeous tonight. I like the way you've pulled your hair up. It shows off your shoulders and that dress... those legs...whew. You're a knockout."

Her cheeks warmed and she resisted the urge to fan herself. "I don't know what you're talking about. You're the one looking like a magazine model."

Delight tickled her stomach as his neck turned deep red, raced up his face, and ended with the tips of his ears. He cocked his jaw, shaking his head. "You stop that. I'm nothing special, but you sure are."

She narrowed her eyes and stepped closer. "Oh, you are most definitely special, Mr. James." Flattening her hands against his chest, she leaned into him. "And especially to me." His heart thundered against her hand, and she grinned.

One eyebrow ticked upward. "You're not playing fair."

"All's fair in love and war, right?" She winked.

"Is that so?" His voice dipped low as his arms wrapped around her. "Then challenge accepted."

Whew. She'd played with fire and now she was getting a little singed. "Uh…I wasn't saying we're at war." The last word came out an octave higher.

He nuzzled her neck with his nose. "I am."

Her eyes closed as she pressed her cheek against his, inhaling his cologne or aftershave or whatever sort of spicy scent he was wearing, and melted into him further. Wow. This man turned her to Jell-O with an ease she wasn't accustomed to.

"Um, are we interrupting anything?" Tim's question shattered the little bubble, and Meesha wanted to throttle him. Not that she wanted to get all handsy in a restaurant, but seriously, couldn't the guy see they were having a moment?

Sawyer held her still. "Well, sorta, but it's okay."

It was definitely not okay with her. Meesha held in a giggle as she straightened. The moment she faced Anna and Tim, she could feel something was off, but couldn't quite put her finger on it. "Everything okay?"

Anna smiled. "Everything's fine. Did you guys have a good time at the beach?"

It took every ounce of control she had to keep her cheeks from flaming. Good time? More like fantastic with that life-altering, entire-drawer-of-socks-on-the-moon kiss they shared. "It was great. How about you guys?"

"It was great until his client tracked us down."

Meesha's jaw dropped. "No way!"

Nodding, Tim exhaled heavily. "Yeah, but I took care of the issue quickly, and this time set some boundaries." He looked at Anna and grinned. "I...need balance—"

Anna held up her finger. "We're engaged!"

Wow, she'd been totally off about the tension between them. "That's fantastic. Congratulations!" She embraced Anna. "I'm so happy for you."

Leaning back, Anna grinned wider. "Thank you."

Sawyer shook Tim's hand. "Congratulations, man. That's great."

"Thanks. I figured I needed to make her mine before she got away." He looked at Anna and winked.

Meesha stepped back, finding the groove of Sawyer's body and fitting herself next to him. "No wonder you wanted to have dinner. An engagement is definitely worth celebrating."

Anna snuggled against Tim. "I'm glad you're not upset with me interrupting your time together."

"No, not at all," Sawyer said. "In fact, dinner will be my treat tonight."

"Parson's party of four?" the Maitre'd called.

Anna bounced on her toes. "Oh, that's so sweet of you. Thank you so much."

"My pleasure. These kinds of things need to be celebrated." He caught Meesha's gaze. "At least I think so."

"Yeah."

As they trailed behind Anna and Tim on the way to the table, Meesha couldn't help but wonder about life with Sawyer. She shook her head, clearing the thoughts. That kiss was amazing, but they were pretending. Plus, as much as she might want more, until he trusted her, there was no point wondering about the future. She'd just have to hope that once this whole thing with Noel was over, Sawyer would give her the chance to show him she didn't give up easily.

16

Stuffing his hands behind his head, Sawyer watched the shadows roll across the ceiling like waves as the ship sailed. Man, what a day. He'd spent the afternoon with Meesha, hanging out at the beach, enjoying her company and soaking in her affection. It'd been his definition of fantastic.

Their little talk had ended much differently than he'd expected. He'd told her he wasn't worthy of her. That she needed to find a man who was, one who would love her. Then the way she'd held his gaze and said she should get a say in who that man was… that an ugly past didn't mean an ugly future…it'd been a little earth shattering for Sawyer. He'd heard her or tried to hear her.

Then she kissed him.

He'd frozen, and the moment he'd made up his mind

he wouldn't let her do it again, she began brushing her lips across his and every ounce of his willpower had exited stage right. He'd taken her face in his hands and kissed her until he couldn't breathe. Even better, she'd been as breathless as he was when he broke the kiss. It was headier than anything he'd ever experienced.

The entire thing had left him confused. What if he *was* the man who was worthy of her or at least could work to be worthy. He knew he could love her, honor her, and cherish her. *Man, he could love her.* He'd pour his heart and soul into building something with her if it meant he'd get to spend his life with her.

Sawyer smiled. She'd fit so perfectly in his arms. A woman had never looked at him the way she looked at him either. It made his heart gallop thinking that she seemed to want him the way he wanted her. It'd been a fun little moment until Tim and Anna interrupted them.

They confused him. While Sawyer was happy for them, their announcement was later overshadowed when they'd talked about going to Magen's Bay instead of Lindquist. It'd almost seemed like Tim had known about the change in plans, too, which sent an odd feeling through Sawyer's gut. By the end of the meal, Sawyer felt much more confident about calling Ryder and asking for more information on the guy.

A leisurely stroll to the ship had given him the quiet he'd needed, and his brain and heart had thrown fists. He was her bodyguard with a past that wasn't just ugly, it was downright mangled. Of course, she'd picked up on it, but she hadn't pushed when he escaped to his bedroom the moment they reached the cabin.

Any thoughts of actually getting to sleep died after he'd tried a multitude of things to get his mind off of her, their talk, and their kisses—and all had failed, leaving him tossing and turning, and now, he was starving.

Stretching, he grabbed the phone and ordered some French fries—his typical go-to when he'd had a queasy stomach, giving them a note that they should keep the knock on the door light since Meesha was mostly likely asleep. Which meant he needed to be closer to the door.

After a quick trip to the bathroom, he made his way to the living room and stopped as he caught sight of Meesha on the balcony outlined by the faint glow of the deck light. He walked to the open French doors. "Uh, hey."

Meesha glanced over her shoulder. "Hey."

"What are you doing up?" he asked as he joined her.

"Woke up and couldn't go back to sleep." She gave him a small smile. "Are you feeling any better?"

He leaned his hip against the railing. "Who said I was feeling bad?"

"You hardly ate your lunch, and then you lost your color while we were walking on the beach. When Tim and Anna suggested we go shopping, you tried to hide it, but I caught the frown on your lips."

Shaking his head, he chuckled. He could get used to the fact that she cared about him. To know he had her attention tickled him to pieces. "Nothing gets by you, does it?" It made his heart tick up a notch that she was watching his lips too.

"Not really. Plus, I was keeping an extra eye on you because of the head injury. If I really cared, we wouldn't have even visited Puerto Plata."

He waved her off. "Nah, my head is fine."

"Maybe, but that garden wiped you out, and I knew it. It was selfish—"

"Stop. I'm a grown man. If I'd wanted to stay on the ship, I would have spoken up."

Her lips quirked up. "No, you wouldn't have. You'd have gone until you dropped if you thought I wanted to do something."

With a chuckle, Sawyer said, "Fine. You have me there, but I promise I'm fine." He nodded toward the door. "I did order something from room service though, but I thought you'd be asleep. I can add to it, if you want."

A wrinkle of her nose and slight shake of her head. "No, I'm okay."

"So, why were you really up?" He'd caught the slight lift of her lips when he shot her a half-smile, so he used what he had in his arsenal in the hopes of getting her to talk.

One eyebrow lifted. "You aren't supposed to be able to read me that well, Mr. James, especially since we just met."

He held up his hands in surrender. "Hey, a fella's gotta do what a fella's gotta do."

With a chuckle, she gave a little one-shoulder shrug and then held up her left hand which sported a small ring. "Noel gave me this at our one-month anniversary. I was so surprised. I mean, I'd dated a couple of times before, maybe a few times in high school and college. None were as attentive and sweet." She turned and faced the railing. "When we'd walk on the sidewalk, he'd make sure I was on his left, so street-bike thieves wouldn't steal my purse. He'd open doors for me. He'd just…do little things that said…" She sighed. "He cared about me. It was so different."

"Then he introduced you to his parents?"

She nodded and then curled her lip. "No, well, yes, but those little things that at first impressed me turned into something else. He wanted to know where I was, what I was doing all the time. Once I met his parents, it was even worse. Actually, I was thinking of ending things right before I met them, but after seeing the way they treated him, I thought maybe if he could see that someone truly cared for him, he'd change. I've never been so wrong in my life."

Sawyer crossed his arms over his chest. "You know none of it's your fault, right?"

"Isn't it?" Her voice rose an octave. "I knew something was off, and I still stayed with him."

His arms dropped to his side. How could she for even a minute think that? "You cared about him, and you have a kind, compassionate heart. Everything he did is on him." How the man could have thrown that away befuddled Sawyer. He'd only a glimpse of the way she took care of people, and despite the knowledge it could go nowhere, it didn't stop him from peeking into the future.

"Yeah, and it got me stalked, fired, and nearly got myself k—" She stopped short. "...hurt worse than I did."

He took her by the shoulders and made her face him. "That wasn't what you were about to say." When she wouldn't look at him, he set his finger under her chin, tilting her head up until their eyes met. "What did he do?"

Meesha chewed her lip. "I've never told anyone. Not a soul. I was too embarrassed."

"I want—" A sound—like the door shutting—stopped him, and he jerked his attention to it. "Did you hear that?"

"It was probably room service knocking on the door."

The door cracked open, and Sawyer stepped in front of Meesha, taking a fighting position. "Stay behind me."

Diana, the concierge they'd met on their first night, poked her head in. "I'm so sorry. I knocked a few times, and no one answered. I didn't want your fries to get cold."

Well, he had given them a note to knock softly, but he'd been listening for the door.

Meesha's hand came to rest on his shoulder. "I think it's okay."

Sawyer hesitated a second and softened his posture a fraction. Just because the concierge was a woman, didn't mean she wasn't a threat.

"I really am sorry. I didn't mean to scare anyone," Diana added. She groaned. "I'm sure you were thinking someone was trying to break in. I should have thought about that."

Maybe he wasn't dividing his attention as much as he thought. It was possible he just didn't hear her. He crossed the distance and opened the door for her. "It's okay. Just caught me off guard." He swung the door wide for her to push the cart in.

Meesha joined Sawyer in the living room. Meesha strolled to a stop next to Sawyer. "Hi, Diana. He gets jumpy sometimes, but I like that he's protective. It makes me feel special." She smiled and wrapped her arms around his bicep.

Nodding, Diana wheeled the cart inside. "That's really sweet. I think all women look for that in a man." She clasped her hands in front of her.

"Have you been enjoying the cruise?" Her head tilted as she looked at Sawyer. "Did something happen?"

"A little mugging at the first port, but I'm okay. Have you heard anything from the authorities about the person who ransacked the cabin?"

Diana's mouth dropped open. "That's awful, and no, we haven't."

Shrugging, Meesha said, "I doubt you will. Plus, nothing was taken, so it was really stupid on their part. I mean, a trip like this isn't cheap to start with, and then add getting arrested, getting fines, or whatever. No thanks."

"You still haven't found anything missing, right?" Diana asked.

Sawyer and Meesha looked at each other. "No, I've

got all my stuff," he said.

Diana nodded to Meesha's finger. "That's a pretty ring." She looked at Sawyer. "You've got good taste."

"Um, thank you." The tone was polite, maybe even coated in a little sadness.

"Well, I should let you guys eat. I'm sure I've got someone wanting my attention." She shuffled back to the door. "If you need anything else, just give the concierge a ring. Have a good night." With that, she walked out of the cabin, shutting the door behind herself.

"That's a lot of French fries." Meesha asked.

"Some people want crackers, Mia likes Doritos, and for me, when I've felt bad, it's fries." He chuckled and caught her gaze. "Now, no more stalling."

"I can wait until you eat, so your fries don't get cold."

He glanced at the cart. "Okay. I'll eat, and you talk."

With a groan, Meesha wilted onto the couch and put her back to the arm. "I just…"

"Talk."

"Fine." She heaved a sigh.

Taking the lid off the fries, the aroma hit his nose and his mouth watered. He grabbed the plate and took a seat on the couch with enough space to set the plate between them. "I don't mind sharing."

They ate in silence for a moment. "I think Kayleigh

and Tru suspected I wasn't telling the whole story. I just didn't want to upset my mom and dad or my sisters."

Sawyer nodded in understanding as he stuffed a couple of fries in his mouth.

"Noel did more than break my door down. He chased me around my apartment, and I almost escaped out a window. But he caught me, and…" She looked down at her hands, swallowed hard, and continued, "He tried to strangle me to death. The only reason the hospital didn't call my family right away was because there was a mix up at the school, and my emergency contact information was missing."

"Meesha…"

She lifted her gaze to his, tiny droplets of tears clung to her lashes and her cheeks were streaked. "I didn't want them to know I'd been so stupid. And… there was nothing they could do. I said I needed to pack, but I was trying to stall so they wouldn't see the bruises on my neck. Once they were no longer visible, I flew home."

"You weren't stupid, and you aren't stupid. You couldn't have predicted that he'd physically assault you. I'm positive that your family will feel the same way too. None of this is your fault. It lies square at Noel's feet."

Shrugging, she said, "Maybe, but it sure feels that

way. All the warnings, all the videos and reports of women finding themselves in a domestic abuse situation…all of it and I let it happen. He broke my self-esteem, my confidence, my discernment. I ignored my gut feeling, and now, it's like I don't know if it's *my* instinct or if it's my fear of letting someone else do to me what Noel did. How can I trust myself?"

Sawyer scooted closer. "Listen, I've done this long enough to know that you need to feel how you want to feel. Just know that caring about someone doesn't make you stupid. It makes you human."

She rubbed her eyes with her hands. "I can't stop crying. I hate myself for still harboring feelings for him, other than anger. And this stupid ring…" She touched it. "It reminds me of how sweet he was and every time I try to throw it away, I can't. I just want to feel like myself again. Happy, unafraid, and confident. Here it is a year later, and the hope that I will ever be that way again, diminishes every day…" A hiccup escaped and then another.

He wrapped his arms around her, pulling her flush against his body, and kissed the top of her head. "I've got you. You cry as much as you want." A second later, he was lifting her onto his lap as she sobbed.

The sweet woman in his arms had shown him more care than he'd ever known, and Noel was never touching her again. Not as long as Sawyer had breath.

17

Meesha woke with a start, quickly realizing that she was on the couch lying next to Sawyer with his arms around her. His chest was rising and falling evenly, and he'd been wrong to say he snored, or it wasn't consistent.

Then the events of the evening before began to flood her mind. She and Sawyer had bowed out of shopping with Tim and Anna. It'd sounded like a load of fun, but she knew Sawyer was tired, and Tim was reminding Meesha of Noel far more than she could handle.

They'd basically returned to the ship and gone straight to their rooms. She'd been physically and mentally spent, and all she did was toss and turn. Hours later, she'd gotten so restless she'd made her way to the balcony intending to throw the ring away, but every time she pulled her arm back to fling it, she'd stopped. Idiot. She was an absolute idiot. After all he'd put her through, and still she clung to the good memories.

She hadn't expected Sawyer to find her on the balcony. He'd looked like he was about to drop by the time they finished walking the beach, and she suspected he'd sleep through the night. He was a little more observant than she realized too, both her reason for being awake and how his lopsided smile affected her.

Telling him about the break-in…what happened with Noel, certainly wasn't planned. She'd held that information so close for so long when she finally began talking about it, she'd lost it.

But Sawyer…

He'd hugged her, then pulled her close, and it'd been more comforting than she'd ever be able to properly express. Even now, she wasn't in a super hurry to get up, even though she had a good suspicion they were missing much of their St. Thomas stop. Then she realized for the first time in a while that she hadn't had any nightmares.

Actually, on the whole, she felt better and lighter. She'd always thought talking about it would only make her relive it, and to a degree it did, but it did so much more than that. She did relive it, but that meant she'd survived it. How many didn't? But she did.

She had a pretty great life too. Myrtle Beach wasn't France, but it was bright and sunny. A fantastic job that she loved. It may not have the prestige that her old school had, but the kids were loving and sweet. Her principal and vice principal were supportive, and they listened.

Why had she kept all that stuff locked inside? Kennedy had told Meesha that she felt stupid for believing her ex would change. Meesha didn't think she was stupid at all. She loved him and he'd changed. How was she supposed to know that the man she loved would turn into an entirely different person just a few years after they married? She couldn't have, and the sad truth was that no one could see the future nearly as clearly as they could see the past.

"Are you always this beautiful when you wake up?" his voice was low and husky.

"You don't even have your eyes open."

"I don't have to." A smile lifted his lips as he opened his eyes. "Do you feel better?"

Nodding, she said, "Actually, I do. Most of the time, I can't sleep through the night. I think this is the first time I've felt somewhat rested in a long time."

He pushed her hair back with his hand. "A good cry will do that, too."

"I think that had more to do with you."

It was soft, but she caught the small catch in his breath. His eyebrows knitted together, his eyes searching hers. "I wish…I wish things were different. If they were…"

"Let's say I agree with you, and that you did something horrible in your past. I can see the anguish in your eyes, and hear the sorrow in your voice. If what happened was entirely your fault, the person you were then is not the person you are now." She quickly added, "And that's only if I believe that you consciously and deliberately did something horrible, which I don't."

"I'm not sure you'd say that if you knew."

She combed her fingers through his hair and then rested her hand on his cheek. "What if you had my promise that it wouldn't matter?"

He held her gaze, and as the silence stretched out, the air grew thick. "I don't think you'd be able to keep it. Not because you break promises but because the sin is too great."

She just didn't believe that. Tru let Sawyer be her bodyguard. Trusted the man enough to let him accompany her on a cruise, putting her thousands of miles away. If Tru even had a doubt about the man holding her, he wouldn't be on the cruise. Sawyer was a good man. Quiet and gentle and brave.

"I see you, Sawyer James. I see all of you. That big heart, the fountain of courage, and selflessness. A man with no honor and no conscious doesn't volunteer to go on a cruise or fake date someone. He doesn't seek out ways to protect people. You do. Your past doesn't have a stranglehold on your future." It didn't have to put one on hers either. The words sank a little deeper and tears stung her eyes. "One bad thing doesn't make you a bad person."

His eyes slid closed, and he pulled her closer. "I want to believe that," he whispered.

Meesha pulled back a fraction and kissed his cheek. "I'll keep saying it until it sinks in."

He chuckled. "Laying here all day is really tempting, but I think if we're going to see St. Thomas, we need to get going." Translation? He was done with the topic and ready to move on to something else.

With a groan, she said, "I've never wanted a clone so bad in my life."

This time, his laugh came from his stomach, and his body shook. He leaned back, kissed her nose, and smiled. "Miss Kingston, I've never liked anyone I've protected as much as I like you."

She pushed up on her elbow and checked the horizon. "I think if we hustle just a little, we can make St. Thomas in time to snorkel. We weren't supposed to port until after noon." She returned her attention to Sawyer. "That's if you're feeling okay."

"I'm fine."

"Okay." She smiled and wished like the dickens she didn't have morning breath. Or maybe it was better she did, otherwise, she'd kiss him and tell St. Thomas to take a hike.

They untangled and stood. "I won't be long," Sawyer said.

"Okay. Meet you back out here."

Once he was in his room, she walked to the balcony and tossed Noel's ring as far as she could. She was officially done carrying him around. It'd been long enough. When she returned to Myrtle Beach, she was living her life without fear. Even if he was trying to stalk her again, she wasn't cowering in fear. She'd meet him face to face, and this time, if he put his hands on her, he'd find out just how much she'd changed.

18

Waist deep in water, Sawyer could now check snorkeling off his bucket list. So far, it had been a blast too. St. Maarten's Mullet Bay beach featured clear water, bright fish, and a variety of corals which made the whole experience one he'd never forget. Sharing the memory with Meesha only enhanced it.

At least he didn't have to thank Tim for this experience. He'd been so odd at dinner the night before and had seemed almost offended they hadn't visited the beach he'd suggested. Eventually, he'd apologized, but it'd still hit Sawyer the wrong way.

Meesha broke the surface of the water, lifted her scuba mask off, and wiped her face. "I've never seen so many fish. It's just beautiful." She slid the mask over her hand, letting it dangle like a bracelet.

Since waking up, it'd seemed like the world had slid off her shoulders. Far different from the night before. Her eyes were brighter, her smile was wider, and she had a glow about her. If possible, it made her even more beautiful.

The ring was missing too. He wasn't sure if she'd tucked it away again or tossed it. If he had to make a bet, he'd guess the latter based on how vibrant she seemed.

"It is, but you give it serious competition." He grinned.

She waved him off. "Flirt."

Sawyer closed the distance. "I'm not."

"Are too," she said. "A huge flirt."

He shot her a lopsided smile. "Nah."

She gave a sharp gasp, pointing her finger at him. "And that right there is *wrong*. You're using your male wiles on me."

"Male wiles?" His head dropped back as he laughed so hard it reached the bottom of his gut. He brought his attention back to her. "That's not a thing. Only women have wiles."

Balling her fists, she set her hands on her hips, tipping her head up so she looked down her nose. "Obviously that's not true or you wouldn't be using my favorite smile against me."

Sawyer closed the rest of the distance and circled

his arms around her waist. "Favorite smile, huh?"

"Like you don't know it." A lone eyebrow lifted as she dropped her arms to her sides and stepped into him. "And two can play at that game." Her hands slid up his chest, and hooked her fingers behind his neck, nuzzling his jaw with her nose. "I've got a list of my favorite things about you, ya know."

He swallowed hard and worked to keep his voice steady. "Uh, you do?"

"Mmmhmmm." She touched her lips to his jaw and skated them along it, pressing feathery kisses every few inches. "Like when your eyes light up when you're happy. How big and strong you are." Her lips reached his and hovered a breath away. "The way you kiss me. Hold me. And especially how adorable you are when you get tongue tied."

Like right at that moment? Because he was. His tongue was stuck to the roof of his mouth, and even if it wasn't, he was so dizzy, he wasn't sure he could form a coherent sentence.

She set her cheek against his and set her lips against his ear, whispering, "It seems as though a cat has scampered away with your tongue once again, Mr. James." Her low, sultry voice tickled, and a shiver ran down his spine. A tiny giggle popped out. "Gonna wield that smile against me again?"

If this is what he got in return? He cleared his throat. "Maybe."

"I see." Her lips parted and she ran them over his cheeks, across his nose, and down to his lips, nipping at them with her teeth.

The warm fire in his belly spread through his body as he caught her lips and deepened the kiss. Whatever space was left disappeared as his arms tightened around her, bringing her flush against his body.

Man, she was soft in all the right places. Her lips were sweet. He didn't feel broken when she looked at him. Even better, she was returning his kiss with what felt like the same passion-filled need. It'd been so long since he'd held and kissed a woman. Maybe that was fueling all of this. Even as the thought entered his mind, he shot it down.

She'd turned around in that conference room, the lights had dimmed, and it was as if God put a spotlight on her, saying she's the one. His head and heart had been in a war ever since. Kissing her was magical, and being with her was a balm to his soul.

What if I said I don't care? The question whispered in his mind. His past was stained with death. As much as he wanted to believe that she wouldn't care, how could she not? Her promise had held conviction, but she could make it as fierce as she wanted when she didn't know his sin. There was no way she could keep her promise if she knew. And kissing her was as wrong as wrong could get because he was kissing her with a future in mind. What scared him most? She was returning his kisses with what felt like the same intention.

Sawyer abruptly pulled away and held her out from him. "I'm sorry," he said, his gaze pinned on the water and his breath labored. "I can't. You don't know."

"Then tell me." It sounded like she was as winded as he was. "I refuse to believe—"

"I murdered someone." He lifted his gaze to hers as he blurted it out. "My bullet. My fault. I killed a civilian. I can't take it back. I can't make it pretty." His hands dropped to his side. "You deserve better. Someone with a clean conscious, or at the very least, cleaner than mine."

Her face fell and she took a step back. "Sawyer—"

That was the only sign he needed to know he was right about any chance they had. He could already hear it. The same words his numerous buddies and counselors spoke. *It was a firefight. It was an accident. It was...* The endless excuses and platitudes fell on deaf ears then, and they would continue to fall on deaf ears.

"Hey, you two!" Anna called a few feet away, waving. Tim followed her and they closed enough distance that she wouldn't need to yell. "We've been looking for you guys." She looked from Sawyer to Meesha. "Is everything okay?"

"Oh yeah." Meesha pulled her gaze from Sawyer's and smiled. "Uh, we got a late start, and figured we'd missed the group. We were pleasantly surprised to find out we could still enjoy some snorkeling."

"Well, when you both seemed so tired yesterday, I thought you might sleep in a little, so I told them to expect you. We wanted to spend the first part of the day checking out the island and then cool off when we got hot."

Tim crossed his arms over his chest. "We maybe toured around half of the island, and I thought I'd melt."

"We don't want to interrupt anything, but…" She looked at Tim. "He did a little research last night and there are a few spots that are off the beaten path with some less-touristy shops and local art. We thought we'd see if you wanted to go too."

Translation? Sawyer wouldn't be alone with Meesha. There wouldn't be the awkward talk where she retreated because she couldn't overlook his past. He'd known that would be the case, but it didn't ease the ache in his heart or how rapidly it was sinking into his core. Worse, he'd foolishly gotten hopes up that maybe…

And he'd been wrong.

"I think it's a great idea," Sawyer said.

Meesha touched is arm. "I think maybe we—"

He covered her hand with his. "Can't pass up an opportunity to really experience the local culture, you know?"

She caught her bottom lip in her teeth and slowly began to nod. "Right." She smiled. "It'll be fun."

"Great!" Anna hooked her arm in Meesha's as they walked ahead of Tim and Sawyer.

Tim wiped his face with his hands. "Between you and me, this has been fun, but I'm ready to go home."

"Eh, as long as Meesha's happy, I'm happy." His lips were moving, the boyfriend spiel was coming out, but his heart was far from it. Home sounded like the best thing in the world at the moment.

At least the secret was out. Meesha knew, and now that she did, it was likely all the kissing would come to an end. No way did she want anything to do with him now. He'd seen that in the way she shrank back.

The moment Meesha's feet hit the sand, she pulled to a stop and smiled. "Anna, I need to talk to Sawyer for just one second. Okay."

"Oh, sure. I'll see ya in a sec."

When her hand clamped down around Sawyers, it was as if she was squeezing a lemon as she pulled him back into the water away from the shore, stopping far enough away that they could have a conversation in private.

"Meesha, it's okay. I'm fine."

"Well, I'm not." She leaned back, crossed her arms over her chest, and cocked her jaw. "You drop something like that on me and then think the conversation is over?"

He set his hands on his hips. "I killed someone. That's the end of the conversation."

Her lips pinched together as her arms dropped to her side. "No, it isn't."

"I saw the look on your face."

"Sawyer, of course I was shocked. That doesn't mean my opinion of you has changed. It means, I needed to digest it a second." She sighed. "I'm still digesting it."

Hanging his head, he said, "I know, and when you're done digesting it, you'll realize this won't work."

Stepping closer, she took his face in her hands. "That's not true. I'm taking my time because if I don't give it the thought it requires, you'll say I'm being impulsive or that I didn't consider it long enough. Not only do I think this will work…I *want* it to work.

"Didn't you hear me? I *killed* someone."

"Loud and clear." She leaned over, looking past him. "I want to continue this conversation when we aren't being watched. Don't shut me out. Just give me time to think. Then we can talk about this again somewhere private and unhurried."

"I don't think location or time will change anything," he replied softly.

She brought her attention back to him and caught his gaze. Her eyes searched his as the silence stretched out. "You're right." She touched her lips to his. "Nothing has changed between us." She took his face in her hands, locking eyes with him. "Nothing has changed. Don't spiral. Okay? Please?"

The war between his head and heart flared again. He could hear the words, her sincerity, but… he also knew that if he fought her, she'd plant her feet and they'd have a discussion he wasn't sure he was ready to have yet.

What if it ended with him watching her walk away? He was broken. His job took him all over the world and it wasn't a desk job. Would she be okay with that? Would he? How could he build a life with her, walk out the door, and maybe never see his family again?

She lifted on her feet and touched her forehead to his. "It'll be okay. We *will* work this out."

His best bet was to plaster on a smile and agree until he could get himself in check. As raged as he felt, his thoughts were even more so. "Okay."

19

Meesha watched Sawyer withdraw more and more with every second. He'd *killed* someone. As far as bombs go, that was up there, but he'd provided no context. Perhaps there was none. Maybe he walked up to someone and ended their life. Her gut immediately balked at that.

There was context and time frame missing to truly make an informed decision. Additionally, she'd made a promise that it wouldn't matter, and she'd made it wondering if it had involved taking someone's life.

"You're lost in thought," Anna said as she hooked her arm through Meesha's. "Everything okay?"

Blinking, she smiled and nodded. "Oh, yeah, just taking in the sights and sounds."

"Are you sure? Sawyer seems upset." Anna looked

over her shoulder, and quickly added. "Not that it's my business, but I see the way he looks at you. I'd be very surprised if you're not engaged in the next few months."

Meesha glanced at Sawyer, his hands stuffed in his pockets, strolling next to Tim. Since the moment they left the beach, she'd caught him staring every time she looked at him. Up to this point, she'd shaken his behavior off, thinking it was just residual jealousy and dislike of Anna, but something was seriously off with him.

She chuckled. "Well, if he does, my answer is yes because I've fallen head over heels for him. I've never felt so wholly safe with a man in my life." The words tumbled from Meesha's tongue with zero effort, nearly choking her. Fallen for him? That was big, especially since she hadn't even dated since Noel.

The thought made her smile though. Made her heart dance in her chest. Gave her goosebumps and tummy flips. She glanced over her shoulder at him, caught his gaze and smiled. He made her want white picket fences, long walks as they held hands, and forever.

With a sigh, Anna said, "Yeah, I can see it in your face." Her lips turned down and she moved a little closer. "Can I tell you something? Something that… never mind it's silly."

Meesha covered Anna's hand with hers. "I don't have a lot of friends, Anna. I've kept to myself for the last three years. I know we don't live close to one another, but I've enjoyed getting to know you. You can tell me anything you want, no matter how silly, and I will listen."

They walked in silence until they reached the end of the block. "I thought I'd be happy getting engaged to Tim, but I'm not. I think the only reason he asked me was because I told him it was over between us."

"I hear you."

"I wanted the foot pop. I wanted my stomach to feel like it was full of champaign bubbles. It just feels… like nothing. I've got this ring on my finger that's a pledge to love, honor, and cherish. He's done none of those things up to this point. What on earth makes me think he'll do those things after *I do*?"

"I'm so sorry."

"It's not your fault I let him basically bully me into saying *yes*."

"Bully you?" It was less a statement and more of a question. "Anna, you don't have to do anything you don't want to do." Meesha took a deep breath, debating whether she should tell Anna about what happened with Noel. It wasn't a story she told many people. In fact, no one in Myrtle Beach knew anything about it. "Can I tell you something?"

Anna smiled. "Absolutely."

With another deep breath, Meesha started from the beginning. Meeting Noel, how great he was, how she'd ignored the red flags, and how it'd ended with her in the hospital. "If your gut is saying this isn't right, listen to it. I ignored mine, and…" She almost said she'd go back and not make the same mistake… "I'm here to tell you, don't ignore yours. Love can be difficult. It's ugly and messy, but it's not abusive. If you've got reservations about Tim, break it off." She quickly added. "I'm sorry. That last part came out as me trying to tell you what to do. I don't mean it that way."

"No, I understood what you meant. I've just put so much energy into the relationship. Maybe this is just a rough patch. He has been stressed at work."

"Stressed or not, no man has a right to treat you badly. Apology or not, if it's a pattern, it's not going to change. And no, you can't change him. Believe me, you can't."

Anna bit her lip, her eyes filled with tears. "I know you're right. I'm just…"

"I hear you, and I totally get it. It's hard to feel like you failed, but you didn't. The relationship didn't work out, that's all. You regroup, do a little soul searching, and then figure out where you want to go next."

She gasped. "How did you know I felt like a failure?"

"Because I did. I thought I could change Noel. I thought if I loved him enough, he'd snap out of it. He was never going—"

A sharp object jabbed into Meesha's kidney, cutting her sentence off. "Just keep walking." A man's gruff voice barked in her ear as he clamped his hand around her arm. "And don't make a scene," he said, jamming the object into her flesh a little harder, making her yelp. With it digging into her skin, she wasn't sure if it was a knife or a gun.

"MEESHA!" Sawyer's voice bellowed from behind. "HEY! STOP!"

"What's going on?" Anna asked and gripped Meesha's arm harder.

Another man joined the one holding Meesha by the arm. He grabbed Anna's arm, twisted it away from Meesha, and pushed her to the ground.

"Move faster." He ground out.

Footsteps pounded behind them, and they pushed her even harder. Scenery was whizzing past her, they were taking lefts, then rights, then lefts and all Meesha could think about was that she was getting further and further away from Sawyer.

The next thing she knew, her purse was being wrenched from her arms as she was being shoved into a building and her hands scraped against the rough flooring as they threw her to the ground. Out of breath and dazed, she looked around, finding herself in what looked like an abandoned coffee shop.

She slowly sat up, her gaze settling on the two men who'd abducted her. The man who held the knife sported blond hair and a long scar that ran from the side of his temple, disappearing beneath the left side of his jaw. Villain number two had chestnut hair and looked like he could take down a lion with his bare hands. The pepper spray had barely worked the last time, and that dude was lanky. It'd most likely turn them into a kicked hornet's nest.

"We wait here." The one holding the knife looked at her and his lips curled. "If he doesn't pay us, we'll get our money a different way."

Her eyes widened as she tried to hold herself together. Her self-defense class had taught her to keep her wits, but they felt like wild mustangs on speed at the moment. The waltz played in her head as she worked to slow her heart so she could focus. "My boyfriend is going to find me and when he does…"

"Shut your mouth," the first thug spat. Was that a French accent?

She held in a gasp. *Noel?* He'd done this? It was the only logical conclusion. Although, how he'd managed to find thugs willing to kidnap her was beyond her. He'd run in circles with politicians and socialites. Granted, it'd been a few years since she'd seen him and there was no telling what he was capable of now. Clearly, he was willing to hire unsavory people to take her at knife point from a crowded street.

The chestnut hair man got two steps before knife guy hauled him back. "Damaged goods don't get full price." He looked at Meesha. "Say another word, and we'll sell you at a discount."

Maybe if she kept them distracted and angry, Sawyer would have the chance to find her. She pinched her lips together and crossed her arms over her chest. "Noel will kill you if you so much as lay a finger on me. He never liked his things being touched," she said, hoping they'd buy the bluff.

Unless Noel had buffed up a lot, these two guys would snap him like a twig. Honestly, as bulky as they were, she questioned Sawyer. The guy was solid muscle, but against these two guys? There was a good chance he might be out gunned.

Both men growled, and the one holding the knife took a step forward just as the door exploded, showering the room with splinters and glass. Immediately, Meesha hit the floor and curled into a ball covering her head with her arms. The very second she was sure it was clear, she pushed up and found one of the men sprawled face down on the ground, holding his head while villain number one was now empty handed.

And there was Sawyer. All he needed was a cape,

some well-placed lighting, and he'd look exactly like Superman. He'd never been more beautiful.

Villain number one roared and charged forward, trading blows with Sawyer. He spun in the air, missing the guy's head and as he ducked, the man thrust his fist up, catching Sawyer in the gut. He hit the wall with his shoulder, grunting. Instantly, he was facing off with the man again, dodging swings.

The guy seemed to have a countermove for every swing or kick Sawyer threw his way. Almost like the guy had studied Sawyer's every move. This time, Sawyer spun around, throwing his leg out and the massive thug caught Sawyer's foot and swung him around, throwing Sawyer a few feet away. He slid to a stop face down and remained motionless for a second. Before the man could reach Sawyer, he pushed off the ground and crouched down, watching the guy advance.

No way could Sawyer continue to take so much abuse. She had to do something. Her phone! She scurried off the ground and scanned the room, finding her purse a few feet away on the other side of chestnut-haired guy who was now trying to sit up. Not only did she need her phone, but she needed her pepper spray. Maybe if she emptied it on him, it'd keep him from joining the fight.

She went to sprint past him, and he grabbed her ankle. Without even thinking, she pulled her foot back and kicked him in the face as hard as she could. The second he let her go, she was scrambling over to her purse, grabbing her phone with one hand and her spray in the other. As she dialed 9-1-1, she returned to the creep on the floor and blasted him with it until there was nothing left.

The man fighting Sawyer slammed him into the wall and looked at her.

Wide-eyed, she spoke into the phone as she kept her gaze on him. "Yes, police... I've been kidnapped and taken to an abandoned coffee shop. We were in the heart of Phillipsburg and these..."

Sawyer took advantage of the distraction, landing several hard punches to the man's abdomen. It almost seemed like he was hitting a punching bag. The man grabbed his fist, forced it down, and whipped his elbow across Sawyer's face, sending him to the floor where he lay still.

"Sawyer!" She lowered the phone from her ear. "I have a whole team of men watching me. If you think—"

"I think I've been following you for two days, and I know that he's all you've got." He snarled. "I think you'll make me way more money if I sell you as an organ donor which means as long as you're whole on the inside, the outside doesn't matter."

Terror seized her heart. This man was going to beat her to a pulp and then sell her on the black market, piece by piece. She swallowed hard and returned the phone to her ear. "If you're still…"

"Duck!" Sawyer screamed.

Meesha threw her arms over her head and crouched down. The next thing she heard was what sounded like bones crunching and a thud. She slowly unfurled herself and looked up.

Sawyer, bloodied and already showing signs of bruising, stood over the man, holding what looked like an espresso machine. "I promised I wouldn't let anything happen to you." The words came out in puffs as his chest heaved. He pitched the machine away, swayed, and she rushed to catch him just as his knees buckled.

"I think I prefer my head in your lap when we're on the beach." He gave a half-hearted smile, and his eyes fluttered shut.

Siren wails grew louder until flashing lights could be seen through the window. Moments later, a flood of police rushed in, surrounding the two men who'd taken her.

She let out a slow breath and curled around Sawyer

a little tighter and touched her cheek to his. He'd saved her life. Whatever had happened in his past, was in his past. She'd do whatever it took to gain his trust, and they'd figure out how to make this work. She was keeping her promise no matter what his story was.

20

Well, this was a smell he knew and hated with a passion. Disinfectant and bactistat, a hospital anti-bacterial soap with a smell he'd never forget. Without even opening his eyes, he could feel that the room was bathed in hospital atmosphere low-light mood. Much like the last time he'd woken up in a hospital, he hurt all over too. That massive goon who took—

He came off the bed like a spring. "Meesha?" His breath caught and he landed on his back with a grunt. Hurt all over didn't seem to encompass the entirety of the body ache he was experiencing.

"I'm here." The words rushed out and a second later, the mattress next to him moved. "I'm here. You need to stay still."

"Are you okay?" he asked through gritted teeth,

cracking his eyes open a fraction to make sure he wasn't hallucinating. That she was actually there, in the flesh. He forced his eyes open further, and her face came into focus. "Cuts—"

"I'm fine, they're superficial." He tried to sit up again, and she set both of her hands lightly on his chest. "Stop. I promise I'm fine." Tears pooled in her eyes. "But I wouldn't have been if it weren't for you."

"Those two goons shouldn't even have had the chance to get their hands on you…if I weren't…" He squeezed his eyes shut. Man, even his eyelids hurt, but nothing compared to the heart hurt he felt. He'd let her down, Tru and Kayleigh down. Everything was down.

Distracted and thinking about a relationship that wasn't even possible in the first place. He'd allowed it to happen, and it shouldn't have. The very second she turned around, he should have taken Tru out of the conference room and… What? Let someone else protect her? Everything inside of him screamed at the very thought of that.

He'd immediately called Ryder and stayed on the phone with him, using her phone to track their location. All he'd seen was red. They'd had the nerve to take his girl, and he was going to get her back or die trying.

His girl. What a joke. He'd killed someone, and now, nearly gotten her killed. If he wasn't batting zero before, he was now. He cut his eyes to the window. Not a lick of light. Talk about a metaphor.

"Look me in the eyes, Sawyer." Her voice was soft and layered with patience. "Please."

She was going to placate him. Tell him that it wasn't his fault that she was taken when it absolutely was his fault. He'd lost her in the crowd. If not for Ryder...

"Please."

He steeled himself and met her eyes.

"Are you going to listen? Not just let the words roll in one ear and out the other?" Her eyes seemed to burrow into his.

"Yeah." But no guarantees. His mental state felt much like his physical state. Broken and bruised.

"Promise me."

Promise? He sighed. "Meesha…"

"Promise me. Because there is no point in talking if you're not going to listen. I need you to actually hear the words." She tapped the spot over his heart. "Feel the words. Do you understand? So I need your promise."

Did she know what she was asking of him? It was his fault she was taken. Fine, she was okay, but he'd failed. Someone had put their hands on her because he was too busy thinking about their beach conversation.

He could also see the intensity in her eyes. When Tru said she would fight for people, he hadn't been joking. *Listen*, the little voice in the back of his mind whispered. He sucked in a shaky breath. "Okay. I promise."

"We were both distracted. I wasn't maintaining awareness of my surroundings, and I suspect you had a few things on your mind. I'm not hurt. A few cuts because of flying debris, but otherwise, I'm good. Yes, it could have turned out worse, but it didn't." She smiled.

Sawyer took stock of the few abrasions on her face, bringing his fingers to her lips. "It shouldn't have happened."

"Maybe but listing out all the things you should have done, doesn't change what happened. Your focus needs to be on the fact that you took on two dudes who outweighed you by a mile. I've never seen men so large in my life. You didn't even hesitate. That door splintered open and there you were like a superhero." Tears overspilled and ran down her cheek. "You could have easily been killed. I'll bet the thought never crossed your mind, did it? Not even once."

At the time? Not really. "Well, not until now." He shifted a little and winced. If he'd had brains, he'd have picked up that coffee machine way sooner than he had. "Feels like they outweighed me too." His eyes widened. "I can't protect you."

"Local law enforcement is standing right outside

until Noah, Ryder, Tru, and Kayleigh can get here. Walker won't be far behind. They're looking into those men and their connection to Noel. I'm safe. You're safe. Everything is okay."

Lowering his gaze, Sawyer's heart sank to his stomach. He'd let Tru and Kayleigh down. He'd promised to keep Meesha safe, given his word. The man was his closest friend and Sawyer had let him down. Meesha deserved so much better than him. "I think...I think we need—"

She lightly touched her fingers to his bruised lips. "Hush. You didn't let anyone down." Leaning forward, she caught his gaze again. "I like the way you protect me. Even more, I like how I feel when you protect me." She paused a moment.

His eyebrows knitted together. "Not only did I kill someone, but I could have gotten you killed too. I'm not..."

"Listening like you promised."

He jerked his gaze back to hers.

One eyebrow cocked, and her lips quirked up on one side. "Well, you're not."

"You're not listening either." He couldn't keep the frustration he was feeling out of his tone. "It's like everything I say just bounces off. I killed one of my best friends. And now this? Are you a glutton for punishment?"

Her head tilted. "Yeah, for you I am."

Sawyer's lips parted as he blinked.

"Tell me what happened. You want me to make an informed decision, right? The only way I can do that is if I know what happened."

As if his heart couldn't sink any lower. Why tell her? The outcome was going to be the same. Then again, there'd be no room for what-ifs later down the road when he was hearing about her getting married, having kids, and living the life she deserved.

Meesha touched her lips to his. "You're safe with me, I promise."

"I was stationed in Syria. It was mostly quiet there with rare conflicts, but there'd been a rise in tension. Skirmishes were kicking up.

"My buddy, Chris, and I were in basic together." He lowered his gaze, smiling. "I hated him. He was this entitled rich kid. Never knew adversity in his life." He grunted a laugh. "Couldn't right? Money didn't buy love, but it could rent it.

"We were assigned to work on organizing supplies, and somehow we got locked in. I blamed him, he blamed me and then the fists flew."

"Oh, wow."

"Yeah, when we were finally out of energy, we looked around and the whole place was torn up. I blamed him, he blamed me. This time we didn't have the energy to come to blows, but we talked trash." He took a deep breath. "Chris's dad was an alcoholic. His mom was doing her best to hold their world together, and he and his two sisters were left to take care of themselves.

"Sure, he'd come from money, but he'd been neglected just the same. It made me realize that I'd been judging people the same way they judged me. I was a hypocrite just like everyone else." A smile greeted Sawyer as he looked up. "We got ourselves up, cleaned up the supply closet, and walked out of there six hours later as best friends."

"Forced bonding usually works." She chuckled.

He smiled. "I guess so. It'd been quiet in Syria. Not many skirmishes, but we had a flare up of activity from ISIS. We were in a firefight with a group of militants. He'd rushed to get some of the civilians off the road and out of harm's way. So, I'm using one of the vehicles as cover, reload, and when I step out to fire, Chris steps in front of me…"

A sharp gasp. "Oh, no."

Nodding, Sawyer dropped his gaze to the sheet tangled at his waist. He could almost feel the heat of the sun cooking him, the smell of dirt and gunfire, and hear the scream that tore from his throat as he watched Chris's body crumple to the ground. "He's gone before I can get to him. I'd killed him. He was just gone.

"The Army did an investigation." Sawyer gritted his teeth. "According to witnesses, an enemy combatant, hiding in one of the homes, had his weapon trained on me. Chris had stepped in front of me to keep me from getting shot."

Sawyer took a deep breath, working to keep his emotions off his face. "They tried to tell me there were two wounds, and that mine didn't kill him. I just…he should be alive. Not me. He was a good guy. Better than I could ever be. He was slow to anger. The first to volunteer. He'd spend his money on toys for the kids in the surrounding villages. Send money home to his sisters." He brought his hands to his face and rubbed his eyes. "It should have been me."

Meesha's arms circled around his neck, and her damp cheek rested against his. All she did was hold him. Unlike any other time, where they'd tell him all sorts of ways it wasn't his fault, she just put her arms around him.

He slowly wrapped his arms around her, crushing her to him, and lost the fight trying to hold everything back. Years of going to therapists hadn't resulted in this sort of release. He wasn't sure how long he held onto her, but by the time he loosened his grip on her, he actually felt…light.

She untangled herself, stood, and when she returned, she held a wet washcloth. Still, not saying a word, she gently wiped his face off. When she finished, she set it on the side table and cleared her throat. She braced her hand on the bed as she leaned across him. "I can't imagine carrying that sort of weight. It had to be gut-wrenching when you realized what happened. I'm so sorry. For him. For you. That the world lost an incredibly kind and generous person."

He stared at him. "You're not going to say it's not my fault?"

"I wasn't there, so I wouldn't know."

"But that's what everyone does."

"I know, but that isn't what you need to hear. You need someone to grieve with you as though you are at fault. Whether they disagree with you or not. Your heart is broken." She brushed her fingers through his hair. "It's okay to have a broken heart."

Was that what he was missing all this time? The permission to be broken-hearted over the loss of his friend? To have the freedom to let his life stand still a second while he processed what happened?

"Would it be okay if I ask you a question? It might be a tough one."

So far, she'd been the only one willing to stand next to him instead of trying to push him from behind. Swallowing hard, he nodded.

"Wait until I'm finished asking the questions, okay? I have more than one."

"Okay."

"Would you have stepped in front of Chris? If so, which I'm guessing the answer is yes, what would you tell him? What would you want his life to look like right now?" Her hand came to rest on his jaw. "What would you say to him?"

The door swished open and Meesha straightened as a nurse stepped inside. "I need to take Mr. James's vitals."

Meesha nodded as she stood. "Okay."

As the nurse took more blood than Sawyer thought necessary, he ruminated over the questions Meesha had asked. Of course, he would have given his life for Chris's. Without hesitation. Sawyer wouldn't want him to live his life in misery either. Not like that'd bring him back anyway.

What would he want for Chris? A blessed life. One filled with a woman who loved him, as many kids as they wanted, and happiness. Fulfillment, prosperity, and a long life. Sawyer's mental trip went full circle. *What would Chris say to him?*

"Wait. What is that?" Meesha asked, snapping him out of his thoughts.

"It's just something the doctor ordered for pain." The woman smiled as she emptied the syringe into the I.V. bag before Sawyer could protest.

Meesha's eyebrows knitted together. "I thought the

doctor said he wanted to see how Sawyer felt when he woke up."

With a shrug, the nurse collected her things. "I'm just following orders. You can ask the doctor during his rotations later today."

Before she got to the door, Sawyer could already feel his body growing sluggish. "Whoa. That hit hard." He struggled to keep his eyes open.

"Yeah," Meesha replied as she sat next to him, leaning over him again. "I'll be here when you wake up. I'm not going anywhere unless you make me."

The world went dark just as she pressed her lips to his.

21

Whatever that nurse gave Sawyer, it'd hit hard and fast. Meesha was still trying to figure out why the doctor would have changed his mind, especially since he'd seemed so confident when he left. The only reason they'd allowed her in the room and given her any information was because of the paperwork they'd filled out before they left North Carolina.

She folded into the chair next to Sawyer's bed and let her head drop back. The last twenty-four hours had worn her out—emotionally, mentally, and physically. It wasn't until she was alone with Sawyer in the hospital room that the shock wore off.

He hadn't even asked about his injuries. Aside from a few stitched cuts on his face, he sported a couple of bruised and fractured ribs. The bruises lining his jaw and torso were deep purple with shades of green intermixed. His body had suffered so much abuse.

A smile ghosted across her lips as her gaze landed on him. He'd told her what happened. If that trust was a physical person, she'd be hugging it. He had no idea how much that meant to her. At first, she thought he'd clamp his lips shut and seal them with liquid nails.

All this time, walking around with that much guilt had to be exhausting. He'd expected her to be like everyone else, but most people didn't have her experience. She didn't want anyone fixing her problems. Mostly, she wanted someone to wrap their arms around her and tell her that it was her fault. She'd made a mistake. To grieve with her the way she needed to grieve.

Of course, dating Noel had red flags, but it wasn't her fault that he turned out to be abusive. Had she made a mistake? Maybe, but at the time, she was doing what she thought was best. Everyone's vision was perfect when they were looking at the past.

A knock came from the door, and it slowly opened. Kayleigh peeked her head in. "Hey." She smiled.

"Hey, when did you land?" Meesha said as she rolled her head.

"Just a bit ago. Tru is helping Noah and Ryder get set up in the hotel. I wanted a minute to visit with you." She lifted her hand, showing off a large paper cup.

"Oh, coffee. You do love me."

Kayleigh made her way across the room, handing Meesha the drink as she said, "Dark as the Mariana Trench," before taking a seat on the bench lining the wall under the large picture window. She tipped her chin in Sawyer's direction. "How's he doing?"

"A lot of pain, but he's okay." She took a tentative sip and then a long drink. "Oh, I needed this."

"You really should get some rest yourself."

Meesha scoffed. "As if you'd leave Tru if he was lying in that bed." She looked at her sister, knowing she couldn't deny it.

Kayleigh rolled her eyes. "Fine."

"He's so sweet. It hurts to see him bruised and battered." She took another long drag of her coffee. When her sister didn't respond, Meesha looked at her. "What?"

"I've seen that look." She rolled her lips in, failing to hide the smile on them.

"Shut up." Sheesh. Sometimes Meesha regretted having such close relationships with her sisters. The way they read each other made it harder to keep secrets. For the most part, she cherished it. "He could have been killed. You saw the photo I texted you, right?" She twisted in her seat, facing Kayleigh.

Her eyes widened as she nodded her head. "Massive. I have no idea how he won that fight, but I'll forever be grateful that he did. They've given up Noel. He's in Puerto Rico. Noah contacted the French Police, who in turn contacted Puerto Rican law enforcement. Ryder tracked him down, so it's only a matter of time before he's in custody."

Relief flooded Meesha and she melted into the chair. A long exhale poured from her. "Oh, that is music to my ears."

"Yeah, they were locally hired thugs."

"Local? Are you sure? One of them had the hint of a French accent."

Kayliegh shrugged. "According to Noah. He's been on the phone with the police a few times. They didn't mention anything about an accent. Passports say they're American."

American? Well, Meesha had been scared witless. Maybe she just imagined it or something. "At least they're locked up too. Maybe this time Noel can get the help he needs."

"And a long prison sentence."

"I won't disagree."

They sat in silence and Meesha knew the next question coming from her sister's mouth before she even asked it. "He did more than just break your door down, didn't he?" It really didn't come out like a question.

Meesha nodded. "Yeah, he did. The reason it took me so long to get things pack up was...I was in the hospital. I didn't want to come home before the bruises were healed."

Kayleigh came off the seat. "What?"

"Shhh."

"Hospital! You were in the hospital and didn't tell us?" she ground out.

Meesha stood, set her coffee on the nightstand, and faced Kayleigh. "I felt so stupid and idiotic. I didn't want mom and dad or you and Autumn to worry. At the time, I just...I was a wreck. I wanted to keep my problems as my problems, especially when you were telling me about your new love. I didn't want to taint that."

Her sister embraced her. "Oh, Meesha, it wouldn't have." She leaned back, tears in her eyes. "I can't believe you didn't tell us. We could have been there for you."

"I know, but I didn't think I deserved it. I'd ignored the gut feeling I had. I blamed myself for the whole thing." She smiled. "But it wasn't my fault. None of it was, and I'm putting the accountability where it belongs—squarely on him."

"Good. That's where it belonged the entire time. The jerk."

With a smile, Meesha nodded and stepped back. "He was. Is." She looked at Sawyer and her grin widened. "I got him out of it though."

Her sister's eyes went wide. "Really?"

"I've fallen so hard for him. He's got such a gentle spirit." She moved closer to the bed and sat next to him, brushing his hair from his face. "He's brave and kind-hearted. It was his idea to come on the trip with me." She sighed and palmed her forehead. "I'd told Anna I was dating someone, and that they were coming with me."

"I know." Her sister's voice was deadpan.

Meesha jerked her head around. "What?"

Her sister leveled her eyes at her. "Ryder. Mia. Like, hello? I didn't know you were saying the guy was your fake boyfriend for the cruise, but they found the dating website."

"I hate your job." She narrowed her eyes. "Don't do that again." Returning her attention to Sawyer, she rolled her eyes. "It was his idea to come on the cruise with me and pretend to be my boyfriend. I even gave him an out on the flight to Miami, and he didn't take it."

"And if you'd accepted the dinner invitation a few months ago, you'd have met him long before now."

"What?" Meesha asked.

"I've been dying to set you up. I love him. He's a great guy, and I had a feeling you'd hit it off." She laughed.

Kayleigh's phone rang and she snatched it out of her purse. "Hey, babe," she said as she put it to her ear. "Yeah, he's doing okay… She is too." Her sister smiled. "Okay, I'll see you in a little while." They said their goodbyes and she dropped her phone back in her purse.

"Go home to your husband."

"No, I'm staying with you. He'll be fine."

"I'm exhausted. I'm going to take a seat in this chair, finish my coffee, and then grab a nap. There's no reason for you to stay." Meesha grabbed her coffee and took a swig. "Eh, cold."

"Not burning the roof of your mouth is not…cold."

A chuckle popped out. "Is to me. Scalding is a comfortable temperature." She softened. "Really, go ahead. It's going to get boring really quick when I fall asleep on you."

Kayleigh eyed her for a moment. "Okay, but you call me when he wakes up and give me an update."

"I will. I promise."

"Don't go anywhere. Walker will be here shortly to take over for the cop sitting outside. If anything feels off, lock the door and call me."

"I'll be fine."

They hugged again, and Kayleigh walked to the door. "I love you, and I'll see you later today."

"Okay."

The door clicked shut as Kayleigh exited and Meesha returned to her seat, coffee in hand. If she didn't have a weird thing about finishing her drink, she'd dump it. What she really wanted to do was stretch out next to Sawyer, but with him being hurt, she didn't want to inadvertently hurt him. She patted the arm. "So the chair it is…"

The policeman stuck his head in, motioning for her. She slowly lowered her coffee to the floor, stood, and crossed the room. Through the small crack, she could see Tim standing next to the cop.

"Do you know this guy?" the man asked.

Nodding Meesha answered, "Yeah, I know him."

"Anna should be here any second." Tim smiled. "We stopped to get you coffee, and as we were carrying it up, she spilled it on herself. She's in the restroom getting cleaned up."

Meesha hesitated.

He stuffed his hands in his pockets. "I can totally wait until Anna gets here if you'd like."

Oh, she felt like a heel. She sighed and backed away from the door. "No, it's okay."

The cop looked at Tim. "You can go in."

He scooted past the man. "Thank you," he said and shut the door behind him.

Over her shoulder, she said, "It's really sweet that you guys got me coffee. Thank you." She stopped next to the chair. Her spine tingled, and the creeps she'd felt earlier returned in full force. "I appreciate it."

"Right." He tucked his hands into his trouser pockets and crossed the room, stopping next to Sawyer's bed. "He's a little worse for wear."

"He saved my life, and he's never looked better. The doctor said his age and fitness will make recovery relatively quick." She slipped her hand into Sawyer's, squeezing it.

"That's good." He tilted his head. "Meesha." Her name floated from his mouth with the same tone Noel used.

She looked at him.

"Do you still not see it?"

"See what?" He flicked on the light, giving her the ability to really see his face. His eyes were… no longer hazel. Her breath caught. "Noel?" But his voice? It was so different.

"Contacts. Plastic surgery. Vocal cords shaved. Plus, a speech teacher." He smiled. "It was a lot of pain, but I'm practically a new man."

She opened her mouth to scream, and quicker than she thought he could move, Noel pulled out a syringe from his pocket and thrust it into the port sitting in Sawyer's vein. "Make so much as a peep, and he'll never wake up."

"Don't." Tears filled her eyes. "Please, don't."

"I won't, but you have to do what I tell you to do." He pulled his phone from his pocket. A short moment later, the nurse from earlier walked in, shutting the door behind her. "Yes, Mr. Parsons?"

"Take this." They quickly switched places and Noel slowly walked around the bed. "I don't want to hurt you. I promise. I just want your help. There's a ball tomorrow night in Paris. My parents will be there and…" His bottom lip quivered. "I just want them to respect me again. Do you remember? They were proud of me. I wasn't a disappointment."

She swallowed hard, trying to find her voice. He'd lost his mind. "Noel, I…"

He charged forward, grabbing her by the arms. "I just need a few hours of your time. The least you could do is give me that after putting me in prison. It was your fault in the first place. I told you. All I wanted was to be a couple again. Just long enough for them to believe it and then dump you. But no, you wouldn't. So, you're going to help me. Do you understand?"

He'd truly lost his mind. Even with her help, his parents weren't going to give him what he wanted. She could also see the wild look in his eyes, and if she said anything, there was a good chance he'd kill Sawyer and her both. "Okay, I'll help you."

"You will?" his eyes flooded with tears. "You'll help me?"

"You aren't going to hurt me, are you?" she asked.

His eyebrows knitted together. "No. You made me do that. I wouldn't have laid a finger on you if you'd just done what I asked you to do."

Her gaze drifted to Sawyer. "And you won't hurt him." She locked eyes with Noel again.

Noel glanced over his shoulder. "What did I tell you?"

"I'll leave as soon as he texts me that you're on your way to France," the nurse said.

Meesha's heart thundered against her ribs. How was anyone going to know what had happened? Where she was? Who had her? There was the coffee. Her sister would know something was up when she found the cup wasn't empty.

"Okay. Yes, I'll help you, but after this…"

His lip curled. "I won't need you anymore. Just make sure it's after we see my parents. Otherwise, you'll force me to do something I don't want to do."

Unstable. Unhinged. Maybe if she kept her cool, played along, she'd give her sister and Guardian Group enough time to find her.

22

Sawyer fought the fog coating his mind, forced his eyes open, and they involuntarily slammed closed again. He'd never felt hit so hard in his life. Minus the guy he'd fought yesterday.

"Hey, man, you need to wake up." It seemed like Noah's voice was miles away. "Sawyer, come on."

The chatter filling his room seemed frenzied and filled with tension.

Sawyer peeled his eyes open again. "Hey."

Tru came into view. "When was the last time you saw Meesha?" asked Tru.

Sawyer sat up, wrapped his arm around his middle, and held in a groan. "I woke up for a little bit during the night, and she was here. Why? Where is she?"

Tru looked at Noah.

"Where is she?" he asked, gathering the blankets

around his waist. He was getting dressed so he could go find her.

Noah set his hand on Sawyer's shoulder. "Whoa. You need to take it easy. Walker and Kayleigh are doing a search of the hospital now. Ryder tried using her phone, but it's either dead or she's turned it off."

There was no way she would have turned her phone off after what happened the previous day.

Sawyer knocked Noah's hand away. "She's my responsibility. I need to find her."

"Slow down," Tru said. "Let's keep our cool. We don't know if anything's wrong yet."

Kayleigh strode through the door. "She's not in the hospital. I searched the bathrooms. Walker got permission to search the basement."

Sawyer worked his jaw. "Is that wrong enough for you?" He looked to the door. "She said a cop was outside. How did she leave if he was sitting outside? He knew to stay close to her right?"

"He was asleep when we got here," Tru replied.

Asleep? What kind of guard falls asleep on the job?

"Did she tell you I was here last night?" Kayleigh asked as she reached Tru. "I visited her last night, but you were asleep."

Panic rose in Sawyer's chest. Just how long had Meesha been missing? "I woke up once, and that must have been before you visited. That was the last time I saw her."

"Do you remember anything else?" Noah left his bedside and joined Ryder at the bench sitting flush against the wall.

Sawyer searched his memory. "While we were talking, a nurse came in to take my vitals. She gave me something in my I.V. bag. Meesha seemed confused because the doctor was going to wait on pain meds until I woke up." He'd been alert one minute and the next he was out. "It was strong whatever she gave me."

Walking to the chair, Kayleigh's eyebrows knitted together as she bent down. When she straightened, she held a coffee cup. "This has coffee in it. She'd never leave a drop of coffee."

Just then, Walker entered the room with an arm around Anna's shoulders. Tears stained her dazed-looking face and dirt covered the soft pink dress she wore. Even from where Sawyer was, he could see her shaking.

"Anna?"

"I found her in the basement, locked in a closet." He looked over his shoulder. "She needs medical treatment, but she wanted to see Sawyer first."

Gritting his teeth, Sawyer pulled the sheets around his waist and stood. "What happened?" he asked as he met her.

Walker dropped his arm from her shoulders and found a nearby wall to lean against.

"Tim said he wanted to see how you and Meesha were, so we came to the hospital. We'd just stepped onto the elevator, and I felt a prick in my neck. The next thing I know, I wake up, tied up in a dark room. I'd screamed for hours, and no one heard me until him." She looked at Walker. "He saved me."

Tim. "Where is he?"

"I don't know. When I woke up my phone was gone and so was my purse."

Sawyer angled himself toward Ryder. "Did you find anything on that guy yet?"

"Find anything?" Anna stepped closer to Sawyer. "Why would you need to find anything." She looked around the room. "And who are all these people?"

He took a deep breath and let it out slowly. "You know I work for a private security firm, but I was providing protection for Meesha because her ex-boyfriend was stalking her. He called her the day prior to the cruise, and I agreed to accompany her, so she didn't have to miss it."

She blinked and rubbed her face. "What does this have to do with Tim?"

Hanging his head, Sawyer wanted to kick himself. The connection between Noel and Tim knitted together. "I could be wrong, but I think Tim is Noel Petit."

"Noel?" He didn't miss the hint of accusation in Kayleigh's tone either.

He looked at Kayleigh. "I'm telling you. Tim looks nothing like Noel. Not even a little bit. Different shaped face, eye color, and height. Meesha said he didn't sound like Noel either."

Tru slipped his arm around Kayleigh's waist. "There's no way he could have known, especially if Meesha didn't know."

She sagged against Tru. "I know." She looked at Sawyer. "I don't blame you."

"You should. It's my fault. The whole thing is my fault, but I'll find her." He infused a level of determination into the words that couldn't be missed.

Kayleigh pushed the coffee cup into Tru's hand and walked to Sawyer. "No, it's not. It's Noel's fault."

It was a nice gesture. A sweet and kind one, but wholly untrue. "Yeah, it is. I was distracted." Plus, he'd been stupid enough to let some random nurse inject his I.V. with an unknown substance. Even Meesha had questioned it, and it'd just floated past him because he was too busy sharing his stupid life story. He'd been stupid and careless.

The conversation he had with Meesha played in his mind. What *would* Chris say if he was standing in the room with him, right that second? The guy would have locked them in a supply closet and chewed Sawyer out.

Chris would call him a coward and say Sawyer was using his friend's death as a way to keep himself safe because he was afraid of becoming like his parents. Only safe had left the station when he met Meesha. He was in. All in. Oh, she was gorgeous. Those eyes and lips. Her soft skin and curvy body. And her heart. Her ability to forgive and let go. The way she looked at him. How her lips would lift in the most incredible smile when she walked into a room and their eyes met. It was like he was the only guy for her.

The feeling was more than mutual. Every time he saw her, he had flashes of future scenes with kids and family vacations and building a solid life together.

"Wait." Anna shook her head. "You were her bodyguard?"

"Yeah," Sawyer answered.

She blinked a few times and tilted her head. "The whole time?"

"Yes," Sawyer replied. "The whole time."

Her gaze locked with his and he knew she knew there was more than bodyguarding going on. If she said a word, after he found Meesha, he'd have to find a hole deep enough to crawl into because the guys would never let him live it down.

"Right...Where *is* Meesha? Where's Tim?"

Ryder raised his hand. "I think I know." Everyone turned their attention to him. "Meesha said his parents were the reason for a lot of his behavior."

"Tim's parents are deceased," Anna said.

"Noel's aren't," Ryder said softly.

Anna stumbled and caught the bed. "Did he lie about everything?"

Sawyer's heart broke for her. To have a man lie and lead her on that way? She came across as a sweet woman, and it wasn't fair that she'd been used like that. Justice needed to find that jerk and fast.

Kayleigh walked to her, put her arm around Anna's shoulders, and nodded. "Yeah, I'm pretty sure he did. I'm so sorry."

She took in a long, shuddering breath. The woman was desperately trying not to fall apart. "Me too."

"There's a huge state dinner tomorrow night. His parents will be there. Meesha said he believed she was the reason they treated him better." He paused a moment. "I think he's got something planned with her and them."

"The French Parliament dinner? The one in Paris?" Anna asked.

Ryder nodded. "That's the one. It's by invitation only. Getting in might be tricky."

"No, it won't." Anna crossed her arms over her chest. It seemed like she'd gone through the five stages of grief in ten seconds. "That jerk thinks he's going to lie to me, abduct my friend, and then think I'm not going to have something to say about it? Oh, he's so wrong." She tilted her head up. "I have tickets to that dinner. I dressed one of the attendees and she loved the dress so much she invited me. That jerk nearly tripped over himself when he found out I'd been invited. The last time he saw the tickets, they were sitting on my coffee table." She grinned. "It'll be so disappointing when he realizes, I hid them in the safe at the back of my closet."

Noah blew out a big breath and raked his hand through his hair. "All right. It looks like we're going to Paris. We can put together a plan on the way there."

Yeah, a plan, and after that plan, Sawyer had his own. The one that included telling her he loved her. If she was willing to put up with him, he'd promise her forever.

23

Meesha cut a glance to Tim. "They'll know that nurse helped you."

Tim smiled. "No, they won't. The security cameras had a malfunction. All they'll know is that Sawyer got an injection for pain. They might question the doctor, but since I paid him too, I doubt he'll say anything."

Her lips parted with a gasp. She knew the nurse and the cop were paid off, but the doctor too? When they'd broken up, he'd been near flat-broke. The only reason they got into the restaurants they did was because of who his parents were.

They reached Meesha's cabin and stopped at the door. "Where are you getting all the money to do this stuff?"

"When I turned thirty-five two years ago, I gained access to a trust my grandparents set up for me."

"Well, then, Anna's going to say something."

"It'll be hard for her to do that locked in a closet in the basement. Just like Sawyer, she got enough sedative to keep her out for at least twelve hours."

Meesha touched her fingers to her lips. "Does she know?"

With a chuckle, Tim shook his head. "No." He pointed to the lock. "Stop stalling. Don't think I'll hesitate to text the nurse."

Anger bubbled in her belly and nearly choked her as she dug out her keycard and stepped inside. All she wanted to do was break his new nose.

"You've got five minutes to get your things. Don't forget your passport either." He took his phone from his pocket. "Don't worry about that blue frock. It's pretty, but you'll need something nicer for the Parliament dinner we're attending."

"Parliament dinner? How on earth did you get tickets?"

"Anna dressed one of the members, and she was invited. When we get to Paris, I'll use my key to pick them up on the way to the dinner. I already had another way in, but it'll be easier with those."

Meesha turned, facing him. "Did you use Anna to get on the cruise?"

"People think I'm stupid. Some French dandy with

no brains, but I've had plenty of time to put this entire plan together. The last detail was you."

A knock came from the door. Hope rose in Meesha's chest. She knew it wasn't Sawyer, but maybe…

Tim walked to it and let it swing open.

"Diana." Meesha smiled. "Uh…"

The woman wrapped her arms around Tim's waist. "I've missed you so much."

"You're participating in this?"

The woman glared at her. "Happily." She gazed up at Tim. "He's been so good to me. When he told me what you did to him, he didn't even have to ask me to help. I volunteered."

Oh, heavens, she was being deceived. "Diana, he's…"

"We met at the hospital. I was a mess, and she took care of me." He bent forward and touched his lips to hers. "I've missed you."

Diana leaned her head against his chest. "We took care of each other."

Tim took Diana's hand and pressed his lips to the back of it. "Would you watch her while I make sure the plane is ready for takeoff? I don't want her to get any grand ideas about escaping."

"I'd be happy to." She pointed to Meesha's cabin. "Go on. Get your stuff." Diana followed Meesha and stayed at the door, leaning on the frame. "Don't take forever either."

Meesha walked to the closet and pulled her suitcase out. What could she do? If she tried to make a break for it, Sawyer could get hurt, and now that Diana was in the mix, how could she leave a breadcrumb without it being seen?

"This is kidnapping, Diana. It's serious."

"Shut up and pack." Diana crossed her arms over her chest. "Your boyfriend, or should I say, bodyguard, won't live very long if you don't."

Jerking her attention to Diana, Meesha said, "What?"

"The lamp. That day I knocked? You two were so wrapped up in what you were doing, you didn't seem to notice the fact that I planted a listening device. Why do you think those two men were as large as they were? Martial arts will only take you so far when the opponent outweighs you by a mile and knows how to evade the moves." She smiled. "The only reason they didn't kill him is because we knew we needed leverage to get you to cooperate."

That's how the guy evaded Sawyer's moves? He'd known about his training. Her heart sank to her shoes as it hit her that they'd learned about more than just Sawyer. Noel heard their conversations the other night. Listened in as she recounted what happened at her apartment, how it'd affected her. She held her midsection as she covered her mouth with her hand. The violation she'd endured back then returned with a vengeance.

"Hurry. Up." Diana straightened and came a little closer. "Noel doesn't want you hurt, but if you mess this up for him, I'll pretend I didn't hear him say that."

Meesha tossed her suitcase onto the bed and began gathering her things. In the bathroom, she hurried around and stopped as she eyed herself in the mirror. "I need to use the restroom."

"You can hold it until we get to the plane."

"I don't think I can." If she could get a second, maybe she could write a note with lipstick somewhere.

Heavier footsteps grew closer. "If you think I'm stupid enough to let you try something, *you're* far crazier than you believe me to be," Tim said and pulled out his phone. "I don't want to hurt you, and I'd really like to avoid hurting your…bodyguard, but if you force my hand, I will make the call."

Bracing her hands on the counter, Meesha nodded and then hung her head. How was she going to be found? Sawyer was out cold. Even if Kayleigh knew something was up, where would they know to look? Tim and Noel were two different people. What were the chances Anna would be found. Even if she was, what was the likelihood that they'd put it together? What if Tim was lying and Anna was in on it too?

Guilt hit her in the chest. Anna had been so sweet to her, and even with their history, Meesha just couldn't see her doing something like this. All she could do now was comply and hope with everything in her that Noah and his team would figure out that Tim was Noel and that he'd kidnapped her.

"Well? Do I need to call?"

"No," she said and straightened. "I'll get packed."

With that, her mind went on autopilot. By the time she was finished, there wasn't a sign that she'd ever even been in the room. There was still hope though. Noah was smart. So were the rest of the guys. Sawyer knew she'd had an off feeling about Tim. Maybe that would be enough.

24

*A*fter returning to North Carolina to pick up Mia, Jax, and Riley, the team flew to Paris. Noah made the argument that if Noel had used drugs on Anna, there might be a chance he'd use them on Meesha. If that was the case, he wanted someone that he trusted to take care of her.

As sick as it made Sawyer, he'd agreed that it was a good call. If Noel had drugged her, she wouldn't be the only one needing medical care. It helped to have Jax along for Sawyer's sake as well. His body had taken a beating, but surprisingly, other than his ribs, he was mostly just bruised and sore. While he wasn't in tiptop shape, it meant he could still participate in the mission.

Once they'd put together that Tim was Noel, they began going over the sequence of events, including how convenient it was that Sawyer was given medication that knocked him out. It'd taken Ryder no time at all to piece together the fact that Noel had bribed the nurse. She'd folded fast too, implicating the doctor and the cop who was on duty.

Luckily for them, Noah was friends with one of the members of the police force, and he would be making sure that Noel wasn't tipped off that they'd figured it out. There was a reason Meesha went with the guy without putting up a fuss, and if Sawyer wagered a guess, it had something to do with him and his safety.

With Anna's gracious offer of her apartment, Ryder and Mia had set up a temporary headquarters in her guestroom. The moment Sawyer stepped inside, he knew it'd been decorated by a designer. Everything was sleek and modern and a mixture of things that worked, but that his brain would have never linked.

"Thank you for letting us use your apartment." Sawyer rolled his head to look at Anna.

He'd watched her ride an emotional rollercoaster on the flight to Paris. His heart hurt for her too. Noel had destroyed her trust, and Sawyer could even see a shift in her confidence. Even when she displayed anger, there seemed to be a lack of conviction, like maybe she held out hope that the whole situation was a misunderstanding.

Curled up on the end of a blindingly white couch, Anna nodded. "I just hope Meesha's safe. I don't have very many friends, at least none who celebrate my successes."

"I'm sure that's hard." He shifted in his seat and controlled his breathing to manage the pain.

"I know it seems like I have a perfect life, but I don't. I moved to Paris right after I began dating Ti… Noel. He made me feel loved like never before." She paused, took a breath, and pinched her lips closed. It seemed she was breathing through the pain too. "How am I ever going to be able to trust anyone ever again?"

Sawyer lowered his gaze. That was a tough situation that he couldn't fully grasp. "I don't know, but Guardian Group has an on-staff counselor. I don't think I'm out of line to offer her services. I'm sure Kennedy would love to help you. She's a really sweet lady who went through her own heartbreak. At the very least, she'll be coming from a place of truly understanding what you're going through."

Noah strode out of the bedroom, crossed the expansive living room, and took a seat opposite of Anna. He was soon joined by the rest of the team with his wife and Kennedy sandwiching Anna between them.

"Are you sure you don't need anything?" asked Kayleigh.

Shaking her head, Anna replied, "No, but thank you. I'm really okay."

Mia looked at her. "It's okay to not be okay. I just want you to know that."

Kayleigh nodded. "Exactly."

Anna smiled. "Thank you. You all have been so kind to me. So, what's the plan?"

Noah looked at Sawyer. "I know the doctor cleared you to leave the hospital, but physically, you are in no shape to go anywhere near Noel." He cut a glance to Mia. "But I know if I try to bench you, I'm going to get grief. So, this is how it'll go. You're going in with Anna as her plus one." Sawyer went to open his mouth and Noah held up a finger. "You are not there to provide muscle. You are there to observe and relay what you see."

Sawyer wanted to protest, but his boss was right. One good hit, and he'd be down, leaving Meesha vulnerable. "Okay."

Tru snorted. "Wow, that guy really did kick the snot out of you."

"Shut. Up."

Walker looked down and away, but Sawyer could see a smirk on his stupid face too.

"My wife managed to break into the guest list and added Tru and Kayleigh, so they'll be going in as well. Walker will be on the wait staff. He'll be able to move around the room unnoticed and offer assistance if needed."

"What about Noel?" asked Anna.

"While we were in the air, I spoke to Kennedy and gave her everything we could about him, including his physical transformation," Noah said. "I just got off the phone with her. She said, based on the information I gave her—and this is me seriously paraphrasing it— we're dealing with a guy who's on the verge of a psychotic break. He thinks Meesha will help him gain the love and affection he's been after since childhood. Once he realizes it's not going to happen, it'll manifest into something either violent where he lashes out or takes it out on himself. So, we should be prepared for either scenario."

Ryder and Mia had taken Sawyer's suggestion that Tim was Noel and run with it. It made sense too. Noel had virtually disappeared off the face of the earth. One minute he was there, the next he was gone.

The guy was smart. He'd been released from custody and disappeared. According to many who knew his parents, they didn't even know where he'd gone. They also didn't seem to be aware that he'd inherited an eight-figure trust fund from his grandparents. Beyond that, the paper trail was spotty. He dealt in cash mostly, which helped keep him under the radar. When he emerged again, he was Tim Parsons, investment manager. That persona had grown and given him access to some of the wealthiest in the world. All in all, the guy had made a name for himself, and Sawyer struggled to understand why he'd put that all at risk just to obtain his parent's favor.

Anna sat forward. "How did I not see any of this? I feel so dumb."

"You're not dumb," Kayleigh said. "Not at all. You trusted him, and he abused that trust."

Shaking his head, Noah replied, "No, you aren't. He was preparing for tonight. There's a good chance we're dealing with dissociative identity disorder."

Anna's jaw dropped. "Multiple personalities?"

"Maybe. That's just based on what Kennedy had to work with. It could be that he was working toward a goal and was able to compartmentalize things to achieve that goal."

Standing, Anna raked her hand through her hair. "I feel like I'm in a nightmare. This is…unbelievable."

Sawyer grunted as he pushed himself out of the chair. "I know. I'm so sorry you're dealing with this."

Her posture softened. "You all have been so kind. Thank you so much."

He palmed her shoulder. "We're going to catch him. Okay? I don't know what will happen beyond that, but at least you'll have that. He'll never have the chance to do this to anyone else, ever again."

Noah stood. "All right. I have a feeling it takes more than thirty minutes to get ready for one of these things so those going to the dinner probably need to start getting ready."

Anna leaned back, a smile lifting her face. Noah had just spoken her language. "I've got it all taken care of. Hair and nails should be here shortly, and I've got a designer friend bringing over tuxes for the men. Ladies, if you'll follow me, we'll go look at dresses."

Mia remained seated as Kayleigh stood.

"Mia, I'd love to dress you as well. Even if you aren't going to the dinner tonight, you'll have something to wow your hubby with when you get back to the states."

"Really?" She grinned.

Anna waved for her to follow. "Yep, I need girl talk."

Sawyer turned to Noah as the girls left the room. "I hope she'll be okay."

"I think she will. It'll take some time, but we'll provide resources if she wants them."

"Walker," Noah said and looked at him. "I want you to canvas the area. There's no way Noel doesn't have accomplices. Once we hear from you, we'll move to phase two of the plan. Okay?"

Walker gave a mock salute, strode to the door, and shut it behind him as he left.

Nervous tension settled in Sawyer's gut. If what Noah said was true, there was no telling how things would play out. If Noel chose to self-destruct, Meesha would be right there to witness it. If he lashed out, she'd be the first casualty. Either way, she was in danger.

A hand came to rest on Sawyer's shoulder. "I really don't think he'll hurt her while he thinks his plan will work, and we've got the area covered," Tru said.

"Yeah, I know." Sawyer swiped a hand down his face. Even getting a few winks on the plane, he was still exhausted. He'd also had the entire flight to second guess himself. Telling her he loved her would be big. It'd be life changing. Just because she seemed interested in him, didn't mean she was thinking in those terms. What if she just wanted a friend? That's not the feeling he got from her, but maybe…

"She likes you."

"What?" Sawyer asked as he brought his gaze to Tru's.

He cocked an eyebrow. "Really? You think I haven't had the same thoughts you're having? I know that look. It's the one questioning everything and wondering if you're on the same page. Tell her how you feel."

"You think Kayleigh will be okay with it?"

A smile lifted his friend's lips. "She's been trying to

set you guys up for months. Meesha kept giving her excuses for why she couldn't come to dinner." He quickly added. "Meesha didn't know you'd be there. We were going to ambush both of you."

"Really?"

Tru took a deep breath and waved for him to follow him. When they reached the opposite side of the apartment, Tru leaned his shoulder against the wall. "Sawyer, I wouldn't have asked you to protect my baby sister if I didn't trust you. Your friend took a bullet for you because you're a good guy. If you were talking to someone in the same position, you'd tell them that even if they were the kill shot, it wasn't their fault."

"I know."

"You know?"

Nodding, Sawyer smiled. "Meesha pretty much said the same thing, and it finally clicked. I've wasted a lot of time and energy carrying that guilt, and the best way to honor Chris's sacrifice is to live a life worthy of being saved. I'd have wanted the same thing for him."

His friend smiled. "It's about time."

Sawyer chuckled and grunted. "Yeah, can't say I'm not hardheaded."

"No disagreement." He straightened. "You hit the showers first since you're broken and will probably take forever."

"Shut up." He laughed and then caught his middle. "That's not cool, man."

Now, all he had to do was rescue the girl, tell her he loved her, and hope that she felt the same and wanted the same things.

25

Being back in Paris brought back a host of emotions, good and bad. Her first walk around the city, the first espresso, the first pastry. Experiencing firsthand all the sights and sounds she'd learned about as a kid. That same magical feeling had returned the moment she'd stepped off the plane and inhaled.

They'd intermixed with the memories involving Noel and by the end, her stomach had soured. Now, he was ruining it again. During the flight, he'd chattered with Diana, whispering with her here and there. Threatening Meesha every so often to make sure she understood that Sawyer's life was hanging in the balance and one wrong step...would mean his last breath. While she was sure Noah and his team had returned to the hospital by now, she couldn't be certain, and she wasn't risking his life.

Her heart ached at the thought that she'd left him there with no explanation, no nothing. What if he woke up and thought she'd left him? She'd seen the doubt in his eyes. The cruise ship was gone. There was no sign, other than a coffee cup, and they had no idea Tim was Noel.

Noel had scared her when he attacked, and now, he flat-out terrified her. One minute he'd seem so in control and the next, it'd be chaos. He'd talk about himself in third person during those episodes. It'd been utterly frightening at times. The worst episode was in Anna's apartment when he couldn't find the tickets to the dinner. He'd picked up a chair to smash a painting, spoken something softly that she couldn't quite catch, and then set the chair down.

They'd left immediately, and before they reached the destination, he'd blindfolded her. He's said he didn't want her getting any ideas about escaping, but as long as Sawyer's life was dependent on her cooperation, she wasn't stepping a toe out of line.

When the blindfold finally came off, she'd found herself at an estate with nothing but rolling hills for miles. Wherever he'd taken her was remote and beautiful. It felt old with its antique, ornate furnishings and tapestries.

She'd spent the day having her nails done and her hair styled. A rack of dresses was brought in varying sizes and shades, all floor length. Part of her wondered if she was going to a parliament dinner or a grand ball with as over the top as it felt. She'd found a few that fit, and Noel had ultimately decided what she'd wear.

Now, flanked by Noel and the same man who'd kidnapped her in St. Maarten off to the left of the stage, Meesha found herself searching the crowd in hopes that she'd see Sawyer, Tru…Kayleigh…someone.

"No funny business." It came out as a gruff bark.

She suspected Noel had bribed someone to get him released from custody. If, by some miracle, Sawyer figured out where she was, he'd come face to face with this guy again. It was an uneven match the first time. This time it'd be downright unfair.

"Noel…" She palmed his arm. It was easy to picture how the events were going to unfold, and the result was going to be a broken man who went through months of pain, only to find out he was never going to get what he wanted.

He glared at her. "Don't speak a word. I *will* text Diana."

Meesha felt like her tongue was cut out. He'd left Diana in the limo that had dropped them off at the parliament dinner with the expressed instructions that she was to remain alert. If she got a text, the nurse in St.

Marteen would inject enough of whatever medication it was into Sawyer's I.V. and he'd never wake up again.

A smile flashed on his lips. "This will work. You'll see."

It wasn't going to work, and anyone observing Noel had to see that his belfry was entirely filled with bats at this point.

A woman who seemed to be in her late fifties, trim, with long salt and pepper hair, styled to the side, stepped to the microphone. Within a mere few words, it was clear that Meesha's French had grown rusty.

Those in attendance clapped, and the woman waved to Noel.

"Join me when I call your name and remember to follow the script."

Noel strutted across the stage, stopped, and embraced the woman. Whatever he spoke into her ear must have been funny because the woman laughed hysterically before leaving the stage.

He clasped his hands in front of him, scanning the crowd with a wide smile on his face until he reached the center-right of the room—his parents—where he launched into a hodge-podge, rambling speech that droned on about his childhood and what it was like for him growing up.

He briefly took his gaze from his parents. "Join me," he said, holding out his hand for Meesha.

When she didn't move quick enough, the thug holding her at gunpoint gave her a small shove. She strolled across the stage, scanning the crowd again. A tiny smile lifted her lips as her gaze landed on a familiar face.

Sawyer. He'd figured it out.

She blinked back tears and took Noel's hand. "Hi, darling."

"Mère. Père. Do you not see? It's Noel."

It was obvious from the looks on their faces they had no idea who was speaking to them. When they continued to look confused, Noel grabbed Meesha by the arm and hauled her off the stage, down the steps, practically dragging her until they reached them.

"Meesha?"

"Mademoiselle Petit."

"What is this?" his father asked.

"It's me. Noel. I'm back. I've done everything you wanted."

His mom tilted her head. "Noel?"

Growing murmurs came from the crowd.

Noel jerked his head up, like he was just realizing there was an audience. "Don't move. There are bombs everywhere."

Bombs? Meesha desperately tried to find Sawyer again and failed. Oh, no. All these people. "Noel?"

"Shut up!" Spittle hit her face. "Just shut up!" He

looked at his parents and launched into French. "We're back together. I helped her get her job at the school back, and she forgave me. We've been dating for months now."

Fear marred his mom's features. "Non." She grabbed for his father, pressing herself into him. "Non."

He rattled off more French, looking from his mom to his dad.

Whatever he'd said had made no difference. His parents recoiled as the shock and disgust on their faces only seemed to grow.

"Mère…" His grip on Meesha loosened. He took his head in both hands. "Non, non, non."

A scuffle caught their attention and someone in the crowd screamed. In the minutes that followed, chaos erupted. Meesha tried to use the diversion and dive away from Noel, but he caught her by the arm again, pulling her flush against him and then held her by the waist as a shield.

"I'll kill her." Noel yelled. "I'll kill her and everyone in here."

Sawyer appeared at the edge of the crowd. "Hi."

Meesha shuddered. "Hi."

Noel tightened his hold on her. "Don't come any closer."

"Noel, you don't want to hurt her. I know you don't."

"I will." The words rushed out. Gasping, Meesha arched away from the sharp tip of a knife.

Sawyer held his hands up. "Wait! You don't want to do this."

His breath hit the back of her neck. "Yes, I think I do."

The next few minutes felt like they moved in slow motion. There was a deafening bang, Meesha was pulled back, and then Noel crumpled to the ground next to her.

A second later, Sawyer had her in his arms with his hand pressed against the back of her head. "I've got you." In one swift motion, he lifted her by the waist, and when her feet touched the ground again, she was standing outside.

He took her face in his hands. "Are you okay? Are you hurt anywhere?"

"I…I'm…I'm fine." The last words slurred as they fell off her tongue and the lights went out.

26

Sawyer pushed out of the chair as Meesha's eyes fluttered open. He'd spent the last few hours waiting for her to wake up. As a precaution, she'd been taken to a nearby hospital for observation.

"Hey," he said.

"Hi."

He brought a straw to her lips, letting her take a few long draws before setting the cup back on the nightstand. "How are you feeling?"

"I think I'm fine. Is Noel…"

"He was shot, but he'll survive. He'll likely spend several years, if not life, in a psychiatric hospital. From what I overheard, his parents completely disowned him. The trust that he'd been using was also revoked. The bombs were a bluff, but he's in a lot of trouble."

Her gaze lowered to the bed. "He was two different people. He'd go from in control to wild and insane in a breath."

"According to what Kennedy told Noah, he may have multiple personalities."

"Oh, poor Anna." Meesha looked up. "Is she okay?"

Nodding, Sawyer said, "Yeah, she's fine. Going through the five stages of grief, but that's understandable. She said she'd be up to visit tomorrow."

"I feel so bad for her."

"I do too, but she's a tough cookie. She's the reason we were able to get everything set up. She let us use her apartment, got us into the dinner. I think with time, she'll be okay."

"How did you put it together?" she asked.

"When Walker came into my room with Anna. Tim had drugged her and put her in a closet in the basement. I'm pretty sure he banked on no one finding her until he'd talked to his parents."

Her eyes went wide. "The nurse drugged you."

"As soon as I figured out Tim was Noel, it was easy to piece things together. When the nurse realized she was in deep trouble, she spilled on the doctor and the cop. They're all facing serious charges."

"The concierge—"

"Diana helped him. Walker found her in the limo a few blocks away. She's in police custody."

"She bugged our cabin." Her lips pinched together.

He chuckled. "Didn't know that, but I'll let Ryder know."

Her lips lifted in a smile.

Bracing his hand on the bed, he grunted. "You'd think it'd be hard to forget that your ribs are sore."

"Lay down with me?" She scooted over and patted the space next to her.

With a little effort, he managed to stretch out next to her. "Whew. Better."

Meesha lifted herself on her elbow and stayed just out of reach. "I just don't want to hurt you."

He slipped his arm around her back and pulled her close. "I'll be okay. I've missed your essence. My heart was in my throat when he pulled that knife. I owe Walker and his marksmanship."

"I was so worried about you. I was afraid you'd wake up and think I took off or something."

"Apparently, you can't leave a coffee cup with a drop of coffee in it."

She laughed. "I've been like that since I first tasted the stuff."

"Kayleigh found your cup, but I knew you wouldn't just leave."

"You did?"

He nodded. "I asked myself what Chris would want me to do. How he'd want me living my life, and I came to the conclusion that I'd been throwing his gift back in his face. If the roles were reversed, I wouldn't want him doing that, so why would he be okay with me doing it?"

Her hands flattened against his chest. "Oh, really?"

"Yeah, and truth be told, it had some to do with my parents too. I'm not my parents though. I'm me."

"Sounds like you talked to someone wise beyond their years." She chuckled.

"I guess you could say that," he said through a laugh. "Oh, I was wrecked when I realized you were gone. That you'd been taken. All I could think was that I had to get to you. I had to tell you that…" He held her gaze.

"Tell me what?" she whispered.

"That I belonged to you the moment you burst into that conference room. You had my heart from the very first second you turned around. That I love you. That I'll work to make this work." He paused. "If you'll have me."

She sucked in a sharp gasp. "I don't believe in love at first sight, or well, I didn't. That day in the conference room it was like my soul found its other half. I've fallen head over heels in love with you. I love your smile and your laughter and your strength and courage. I love you with all my heart."

Her hand came to rest on his cheek as she bent forward and touched her lips to his. "You're all I want, Sawyer."

"You can have all of me for as long as you want."

EPILOGUE

Christmas the next year...

Meesha dropped her fork to her plate. "If I eat one more bite, I'll burst."

She and Sawyer had flown to be with her parents for the holidays, just like the year before. Of course, the moment she introduced him, they'd hit it off, like he'd been a missing piece of the family. They seemed to love him as much as she did.

Once they'd returned from Paris, they'd began dating. The two-hour drive between Myrtle Beach and North Carolina had grown longer than they liked after eight months, and he'd moved to Myrtle Beach to be closer to her.

She'd resumed her counseling with Kennedy. Being kidnapped was no small thing, and since Meesha hadn't told her everything that happened when Noel

Epilogue

attacked her, that'd been part of the discussions as well. It'd made a huge difference in her life, too. She was now able to drive at night.

Noel had survived the gunshot. To no one's shock, he'd been declared mentally unfit to stand trial, and he'd been remanded to a psychiatric hospital. Diana, on the other hand, was still awaiting trial for her participation. Not only that, but the cruise line had pressed charges for breaking into guest's rooms and planting a listening device.

Sawyer eyed the last bite of roll in his hand. "I just…"

"You'll regret it. Remember Thanksgiving? Your stomach hurt the rest of the night."

"But…it's your granny's roll. They're like little clouds of love. It's wrong not to eat it."

Her granny snickered. "You goofy boy. Put that thing down."

"But…"

"I'll make you some more at the beginning of the year."

With a heavy sigh, he slowly lowered the bite to his plate. "I guess it's better that I don't." He looked at her dad, smiling.

"Time?"

"I think so."

Epilogue

Meesha looked from Sawyer to her dad and back to Sawyer. "Time for what?"

Sawyer's chair scraped the ground as he stood. "Time for this," he said, dropping to one knee as he pulled a small, blue velvet box from his jean pocket. He flipped it open and the brightest, most sparkling diamond sat in the center.

Gasping, Meesha's eyes widened. She'd known they'd eventually get married, they'd even discussed in recent weeks, going so far as to look… "That's why we were looking at rings!"

His lips lifted in a knee-weakening smile. "That's why."

"Oh, you."

"Oh, you." The laughter died. "You were the sunshine I didn't know I was missing. I didn't know I could love someone as deeply as I love you. Your laughter is music to my ears and a balm to my soul. Your kindness chases away my darkness. Your heart. Oh, my love, your heart. Your heart is the most beautiful thing. I love the way you look at me. I love the way you want me. I love the way you love me. I love you with every fiber of my being. Would you please be my wife?"

Tears streamed down her face as her head bobbed. "Yes. Yes, tomorrow." She dove out of her chair, wrapping her arms around his neck. "Yes, yes, yes. A billion times, yes."

They rocked back and forth a moment and Sawyer leaned back. He took her arm from around his neck and slipped the ring on. "Can't tomorrow, but maybe Monday." He laughed.

She took his face in her hands and kissed him. "I love you, Sawyer James."

"Meesha Kingston, you own my heart. I love you."

For a list of all books by Bree Livingston, please visit her website at www.breelivingston.com.

ABOUT THE AUTHOR

Bree Livingston lives in the West Texas Panhandle with her husband, children, and cats. She'd have a dog, but they took a vote and the cats won. Not in numbers, but attitude. They wouldn't even debate. They just leveled their little beady eyes at her and that was all it took for her to nix getting a dog. Her hobbies include...nothing because she writes all the time.

She loves carbs, but the love ends there. No, that's not true. The love usually winds up on her hips which is why she loves writing romance. The love in the pages of her books are sweet and clean, and they definitely don't add pounds when you step on the scale. Unless of course, you're actually holding a Kindle while you're weighing. Put the Kindle down and try again. Also, the cookie because that could be the problem too. She knows from experience.

Join her mailing list to be the first to find out publishing news, contests, and more by going to her website at https://www.breelivingston.com.

Printed in Great Britain
by Amazon